The Last
Adventure Box

by

JIM AND CHERYL PAHZ

The Last Adventure Box is a novel and a work of fiction. Any similarity of the characters to people living or dead is coincidental and unintentional.

The Writers' Collective
Mount Pleasant, Michigan

ISBN - 978-0-9886423-0-0

BOOKS BY JIM AND CHERYL PAHZ

Almost Chosen...Nearly Saved

McAngel

Finding Quetzal

Robin Sees A Song

These fine books are available at
Amazon.com

For
Kevin, Erik & Josh
Who Provide Us With Many Adventures
And For
Elida & Gilder
Who Make the Adventures Possible

Chapter 1

DORA

The streets ran on a grid system. Those going north and south were unobstructed, while the east and west intersections had stop signs. Dora was aware of all the traffic signs on the route home; she had traveled this road thousands of times. Each swaying tree, country mailbox, and quirky lawn ornament was as familiar to her as the layout of Sam's Club, where she had just finished shopping. She was, however, on the lookout for deer. Although it was still early, Dora had recently noticed deer along this road at odd times— times when she wouldn't ordinarily expect to see them. She had just remarked about this to her husband, Matt, at breakfast, and he agreed. "Keep your eyes open. I have seen them too, and if you hit one it will really tear your car up."

As Dora scanned for deer, she went through a mental checklist of all she had to do. It would be a busy day. She needed to put groceries away, and then get dinner into the crock pot. If she cooked the meal on high, it should be fine. Her shift at hospice started at 3:00 p.m. and ran until 6:00p.m. That would be enough volunteer work for one day. She should be home by 6:30 p.m. Sarah (her daughter) was out for the night, so Dora and Matt would eat the pot roast by themselves around 7:00.p.m. That was a little late for Matt, but he understood how Dora felt about her volunteer work. He knew it was important to her, so he didn't complain.

Dora smiled when she thought of Matt. He was such a sweetheart, even after 22 years of marriage. It had been Matt's idea to buy the Prius, and when he saw how much Dora liked it, Matt insisted the car be hers. She had never been attached to a car before, not until the Prius. However, she sometimes forgot she didn't need to insert a key to turn on the ignition. And the car was so quiet in battery mode that she had twice forgotten to turn off the engine. Once the car had stayed on all night in the driveway! She was surprised it didn't drain the battery completely. *I am either getting old or stupid,* she thought, *or maybe both.*

Dora prided herself on being a good driver. She drove defensively, and had never had a traffic ticket—not one. She drove past the abandoned one-room schoolhouse on her right, and knew that up ahead would be the familiar herd of cows lounging in the field as predictable as statues. It was a perfect day for taking it easy. The sky was a bluebird blue with only occasional clouds resembling giant puffs of popcorn to interrupt its beauty. There weren't many cars on the road, which was how Dora liked it. She enjoyed living in a place where a person could drive from point A to point B without traffic congestion.

It was different than when she lived on Long Island. She had grown up there and attended the C. W. Post campus of Long Island University. Long Island was congested. If you wanted to go into Manhattan, you had to strategize when to come and go or risk getting stuck on the Long Island Expressway—like an insect caught on flypaper. Dora still had friends and family in New York, and returned there occasionally to visit. Whenever she did, she was greeted with sympathy, as if she were a refugee on leave from some third-world country. She knew people in New York who adamantly insisted they could never live anywhere but Manhattan. According to those people, there was nothing outside of The Big Apple that was worth seeing. The Midwest was a foreign country to them and offered nothing to stimulate the mind. It was devoid of culture. Why should they go elsewhere when the best of everything was in New York?

Dora wondered what they meant by "best." Was it the best traffic congestion? Or the best overpriced housing? Maybe they would miss the best restaurants or theatres? Half the people she knew in Manhattan didn't even own a car because they couldn't afford to park it! They couldn't leave the city even if they wanted to, but they refused to feel trapped. Instead they consoled themselves with the belief that they were living a green (and therefore better) life, even if it made shopping for their toilet paper inconvenient.

Dora didn't feel the least bit guilty as she breathed in the fresh country air and sailed along the country roads in her Toyota Prius. It was full of groceries, Snapple, chicken feed, and a month's supply of toilet paper. She was certain that if she took some of her reluctant relatives and plopped them down in the middle of the mitten, they'd be amazed to discover that civilization exists outside of New York. Once they got over their initial shock and realized how they over-paid for most things, they might actually like it in Michigan. They might even want to stay. Dora shuddered at the thought, as she imagined the people of New York stampeding towards Mount Pleasant. She didn't want her community overpopulated or bloated with its own sense of importance. The town was already growing faster than Dora was comfortable with. She had no desire to extol the virtues of her city. It was a well-kept secret. Dora didn't need or want the best. Right now everything in her life was good, and that was enough for Dora.

There is a lot to offer in Mount Pleasant, Dora thought. To prove her contention, she started counting the number and types of restaurants. There were five Chinese restaurants, two Italian—not counting pizza parlors, and every type of fast food establishment one could think of, as well as chain restaurants like Applebee's, Ruby

Tuesday, Culvers and others. As her mind wandered, she noticed in her peripheral vision a car coming from the west. It was to her right and moving at a fast rate of speed, but she was confident it would slow down and stop. Why? Because that's what the driver was supposed to do, what good drivers did. She knew he had a stop sign ahead, beyond the black mailbox with a horse silhouette on top. She also knew she had the right of way and didn't have to stop. She saw the sign as she approached the intersection. Everything was crystal clear. And then time itself appeared to downshift and proceed as if she were in a dream sequence being filmed in slow motion. Dora's last thoughts were: *this can't happen to me. I'm a good driver. He's not stopping. He's going to hit me!* All these thoughts occurred simultaneously, followed by a thunderous crash. Dora heard screeching tires and the moan of metal being crushed. Then there was nothing—only the void, and total blackness.

Chapter 2

JESSICA

"An orthopedic surgeon—that's the ticket."

Josh didn't hear. He was listening to music by the *Black Eyed Peas*, oblivious to Jessica's chatter. He wasn't much for small talk in the car, and preferred to zone out when he was driving. Jessica loved to talk, so the only way Josh could find peace when he was in the car with her was to play his music.

But the music stopped abruptly just as Josh braked for a stop light. He was startled out of his comfortable cocoon, and felt annoyed. A squabble was sure to follow.

"You might have asked," he said. "I was enjoying the music."

"I'm sick of the noise. It bothers me, and I'm getting a headache. Why don't you put your headphones on if you want to listen so much? You're shutting me out. Is that what you want, to shut me out?"

"No, Jess, of course not. You know I don't mean it that way; I'm just tired. What were you saying about surgery?"

"I said, an orthopedic surgeon is what you should be."

"And why is that?"

Now that she had his attention, Jessica turned toward him in her seat. Josh noted that her headache must have improved because she was animated and her eyes twinkled with excitement. "Because they make the most money!"

Josh smiled. "Really. How do you know that?"

"I googled it," Jessica replied. "And then I discussed it with Daddy."

"Oh," Josh nodded. "That would make sense if all I was interested in was making money. But you know that's not why I chose medicine. I want to make a difference, Jessica, to really do something important with my life. I'd also like to travel before settling down. Maybe I could volunteer for an organization like Doctors Without Borders. I've always been interested in infectious diseases. With your teaching degree, you and I would make a great team. Just think of the experiences we could have, and all the kids we could help. It would be an adventure."

Jessica looked positively stricken, as if Josh had slapped her face. "Josh!" she wailed, "You *can't* do that. Diseases are nasty and besides, who wants to live in a foreign country? You've always had a lot of weird ideas, but I thought you were joking. You are kidding, aren't you? What about our kids, Josh? Do you really want to raise our children in some third-world, back-water hell-hole?"

The twinkle was gone from her eyes, replaced by storm clouds. The traffic light changed, and Josh gratefully returned his attention to the road.

"Jesus, Jessica. We don't have children. We're not even married yet."

Jessica turned away from him and slumped down in her seat with her arms folded firmly across her chest. She was pouting. After a few moments of silence Josh queried, "Do you mind if I listen to music now?"

Jessica sighed. "Joshua, I told you, if you

must listen to music, put your headphones on. Is that too much to ask? You've given me a headache."

"Okay, fine, but can you get them out of the console and set it up for me? I can't hook up the device while I'm driving."

As Jessica fumbled with the wires, Josh tried to calm down and put his irritation aside. He was tired, and Jessica was just being Jessica. When he was in a good mood he found her impulsive, childlike behavior endearing; but on occasions like this, when he was under pressure, he regarded her as spoiled and self-centered. Throughout it all, whether being cute or irritating, she was a stunningly attractive woman. *Beautiful, but outrageous,* he thought. At moments like this he struggled with his feelings. Did he really love Jessica, or was he just enthralled by the sheer force of her presence? He'd never met a woman like her before. She reminded him of the childhood poem about the little girl with the curl, and the ending where it said: *when she was good she was very, very good; but when she was bad she was horrid.* That was Jessica in a nutshell. Then there was her father, who just happened to be his mentor, Dr. Cabot. *Where would I be without her dad?*

As if reading his mind, Jessica said, "Daddy says you can do anything you set your mind to, Josh. You have more potential than any student he's worked with. So don't you think it's important that you choose wisely?"

"Jessica, I haven't even graduated. There's plenty of time to decide upon a specialty. But you know I like travel and I enjoy being outdoors. Other countries might have exotic surroundings where I can be close to nature."

"I hate nature!"

Josh laughed. "Don't be silly, Jessica. Nobody hates nature."

"I do. What's so good about nature anyway? It's filled with bugs and parasites, and dirty things. Where do you think the germs come from? I don't want any part of it, and I'm sure Daddy feels the same way."

Jessica handed him the headphones, and Joshua put them on, relieved to escape once again into his music. He thought of Jessica's father, a former anesthesiologist and Dean of the Medical School. He played a big role in Joshua getting accepted. Josh was appreciative. Jessica's dad believed in Josh and took him under his wing. Without the support of Dr. Cabot, Josh would likely be attending San Carlos University in Guatemala City. Josh was determined to become a doctor, and since he was fluent in Spanish, San Carlos had always been a backup plan. But the backup wasn't necessary because of Dr. Stanley Cabot and the pull he had with the university. Josh was able to get a scholarship and now attended medical school in Florida.

Then, when Josh started going out with Dr. Cabot's daughter, Jessica, Josh believed he must have died and gone to heaven. Everything seemed perfect. Dr. Cabot was skeptical when he learned they were dating. He shook his head and said, "You're studying and dating Jessica at the same time? You must be a glutton for punishment. Seriously, Josh, don't make things too difficult on yourself. Medical school is tough. Even after you graduate, you won't be able to figure Jessica out. I've spoiled her rotten. Believe me, she can be impossible." After three years, Josh was beginning to think her father had been a prophet.

Jessica reached into her purse, removed her compact and examined her face.

"Do you think my lipstick is too red?" she

asked.

"What?" Josh yelled. "What about lipstick?"

Jessica reached out and lowered the volume on the iPod. "I said, do you think my lipstick is too red?"

"Too red for what? I think your lipstick's fine—very pretty."

"I don't know about the color. I'm not sure this shade is good for me."

"It's fine."

"Josh... you act like you don't care! This is important."

"I know it's important to you, but what do I know about lipstick? You're beautiful; you'll look good in any color." Josh paused to reflect. "Why waste time worrying about lipstick at all? If you want to worry about something, what about worrying about Iran? Are they going to develop nuclear capability? Or the Middle East and whether or not conflict will ever end there. Worry about the economy, or unemployment, or housing foreclosures. There are a lot of real important things you can worry about. Be thankful you even have lipstick! There are people here in Florida who are homeless and hungry. Have you heard about Slab City in California?

Do you ever watch the news? The world's a mess, Jessica, and I don't think the color of your lipstick will make any difference."

Jessica hung her head and pouted. "Maybe not, but it's important to me. And yes, I do watch the news—sometimes. But honestly, Josh, the news is disappointing. I can't do anything about Iran, or the homeless, or Slab City or whatever. Is it really going to help if I sit and worry about refugees or people with AIDS, or starving children in Africa? The fact is, I'm a sensitive person and if I think about that stuff I get depressed. So why do it? I'd rather keep my mind on positive, uplifting things, or people I care about, like you, and my family. And, to me, the color of my lipstick is important, because lipstick makes me happy. Honestly, Josh, sometimes I don't know how I put up with you."

"It's a puzzle," Josh answered sarcastically. He reached out and turned up the volume again.

Jessica returned her compact to her purse. Then she pulled out an emery board and began to file her fingernails.

Chapter 3

THE DREAM

I must get out of here. Dora searched while awareness began to come on gradually. *This must be a dream.* There were things – strange, weird shapes – that floated before her eyes. Everything was tinted in greens and purples, and shrouded in some kind of mist. Colors merged together and swirled around her. A yellow amoeba drifted by, followed by a distorted face—no body, just the face. Dora couldn't tell if her eyes were open or shut.

Behind her she heard a quacking noise like a duck and a whirring sound like a propeller or large fan. Disoriented and confused, Dora began to walk and tried to get her bearings. She didn't know which way to go, so she headed toward a faint glow in the distance. The duck sounds seemed to surround her, and she couldn't tell if she was moving away or toward them. She felt cold.

"Not that way," said a voice. She sensed an old man. He emerged in front of her, blocking the path. She couldn't see him clearly; he was blurred and fuzzy. His features were non-distinguishable and kept shifting, but the voice was pleasant, assuring. Dora felt relief. She was glad to have company. The man raised his arm and pointed back to the direction from which she had come. "Over there, you want to go in that direction, away from the light."

"Are you sure?" Dora asked. Her voice was distorted, and seemed to come out in slow motion. She could see her words float and then dissolve, like smoke on a breeze.

"Yes," he answered. She strained to understand him. It wasn't so much actual words she heard, but more like a voice in her head.

"All right," she said. She turned and moved away from the light. The fuzzy man stayed beside her. She felt safe by his side, and warm.

Chapter 4

THE PACKAGE

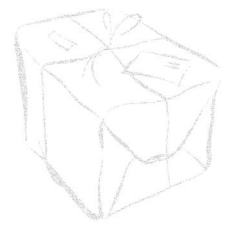

When Josh opened the door, Jessica was standing outside trying to shield herself from the sudden downpour of rain. "My hair," she squealed. "It'll be ruined."

Joshua ushered Jessica into the foyer. She was dripping wet. "I'll get you a towel."

"I should have brought my umbrella," Jessica said, "I don't know what I was thinking. But I was in a hurry to see your surprise. What kind of a box did you call it?"

Josh appeared with a blue towel. "The UPS man delivered it. At first I thought it was videos I ordered from Amazon, the ones you asked me to buy. But then I looked and I couldn't believe my eyes. Come here." He led her into the dining room. On the mahogany table was a non-descript brown box. On the side was written: Adventure Box.

"I got an Adventure Box," Josh said, smiling triumphantly. He was beaming with pleasure.

"A what?"

"An Adventure Box. It came from Gumpy."

"Who's that, one of the seven dwarfs?"

"No." Josh didn't appreciate the humor. "Gumpy is my grandfather."

"Oh. What's an Adventure Box?"

"Something special and this one might be the most special of all. Sit down and I'll make a pot of tea. Then I'll explain."

At the table Jessica fluffed and dabbed her long blond hair while she waited for Josh to bring the tea. Wet and disheveled, she was still striking. Even as a young girl she had been interested in makeup and fashion, and there wasn't a beauty technique that Jessica hadn't mastered. She had majored in home economics at Georgia Southern University in Statesboro where she had also been head cheerleader. Now she was working on getting her teaching certificate in elementary education. With her coiffed hair, impeccable makeup, and stylish apparel, Jessica was

"Barbie" come to life. But maintaining her beauty was time consuming. The makeup alone took 30 minutes, and then there was the hair to manage—color, trimming, styling, and on and on. Once she finally achieved perfection for the day, she didn't want to be messed with or engage in an activity that would undo it all. Whatever this Adventure Box thing was, she hoped it was worth the indignity of the soaking she had just received. She was refreshing her makeup when Josh returned with the teapot and poured them each a cup. He sat at the table and began his story.

"When I was little, my brothers and I were very close with our grandfather. He got the name Gumpy because Erik couldn't say *Grandpa*. Every time he tried to say *Grandpa*, it came out as *Gumpy*. Eventually the name stuck. A couple of years later when I started to talk, Gumpy was one of the first words I tried to say. Even Kevin, the oldest of us, called him Gumpy. The name just seemed to fit.

"Each week Gumpy would take my brothers and me for what he called an Adventure Day. We saw our grandfather practically every day, but Adventure Day was different;

it was our special day. On Adventure Day, Gumpy would plan something exciting like horseback riding, a movie, or a visit to a fish store—the sort of things little boys love to do.

"When Erik was 11 and I was 9, my parents decided to leave Michigan and move here to Florida. Kevin stayed in Michigan that year to finish his last year of high school. He wanted to graduate with his friends. It was hard for me and Erik to leave Michigan because we were leaving our school, and friends, and the only world we had known. But it was especially hard because we were leaving our best friend—our grandfather. We played with Gumpy every day, and he and Grandma were the only babysitters we knew. And, of course, in Florida there would be no more Adventure Days.

"Well, a few months after we were settled in our new home, a parcel arrived in the mail. On the side of the box it read *October Adventure Box*. The next month we got a *November Adventure Box*. For a couple of years we would receive one box each month—just like clockwork. Gumpy took our Adventure Day and packed it in a container for us."

"What was in the boxes?" Jessica asked.

"All kinds of stuff, and never the same thing twice—with the exception of yo-yos. Through the years, we got a lot of yo-yos. But mostly the boxes contained trinkets: a paddle with a ball on a rubber band, a skull made of glass, movies, books, musical instruments, various kinds of candy. During holidays we often got food items like cheeses and sausages, or special sweets like Marzipan and caramel-coated popcorn. But most of the time it was books and toys. There was nothing of great value, but Erik and I looked forward each month to our Adventure Box. The anticipation was probably better than the actual contents. For us it didn't really matter what was in the box; it was always a treasure. It was like Christmas, twelve times a year.

"Are you telling me you've been getting an Adventure Box every month since you were in elementary school?"

"Almost. As we got older the frequency of our boxes diminished. The year I was fifteen we received only three boxes. By the time Erik and I were in college we were getting only two boxes each year. But we never went a single year, since the time we moved, without receiving at least one box. That is until last year—the year our grandfather passed away."

"That's a sweet story," Jessica said. "It sounds like your Grandfather loved you guys a lot."

"Yeah, he did. That's a given. And we loved him."

"So did you open the box yet? Do you know what's in it? Maybe it's something valuable."

"No, I don't want to open it without Erik. The Adventure Boxes were meant for both of us. It wouldn't feel right to open it alone. I've called Erik and he's planning to come here after work. It'll be a few hours before he's off."

"That's an interesting story. Have you called your grandmother to see if she sent the box?"

"I would have if she was alive, but she predeceased my grandpa by six months. They were married more than 50 years. They spent their last years together in a retirement village in Michigan, a place for active and not-so-active seniors. I guess after she passed away, maybe he didn't feel he had much reason to go on. He had a stroke."

"Did Kevin ever get an Adventure Box?"

"No, but that's because he was older than Erik and me, and he stayed in Michigan. Kevin never really left Gumpy."

"Was that fair?"

"Yeah, I think so. Gumpy did other things for Kevin. I know he got to see a lot more movies, and Gumpy sometimes let Kevin use his car. I know Gumpy loved Kevin as much as he did Erik and me, and I don't think Kevin ever resented not getting a box."

"Joshua, I'd really like to be here when you open your box. Do you think that would be all right? I'm curious about what's inside. Who knows? There might be cash, or stock certificates, or jewelry."

"Jessica," Joshua replied, "no matter what's inside, to Erik and me it will be valuable. Maybe not in the way you're thinking, but nevertheless valuable. It will be important to us because it's from our Gumpy, and he's been gone now for over a year. But of course, you can be here when we open the box. We are engaged; so you're practically part of my family."

Jessica smiled, and Josh reached for her hand. Her hair was beginning to dry, but the towel had left it in chaos—a riot of waves and unruly strands. He knew Jessica would hate the way she looked, but he loved her this way, when she was being natural and spontaneous. He wished she'd let her hair loose more often.

"I really need to study, Jess. I've got an important exam in a couple days. Why don't you go home and wait? I'll call you as soon as Erik arrives."

"Ok, honey. I'll leave soon. But first let's finish our tea. Maybe the rain will stop. I love listening to you talk about your grandfather. Please tell me more about Gumpy."

"Gumpy." Joshua paused, momentarily stumped by the task of describing his grandfather. "What can I tell you about Gumpy?" He took a sip of hot tea, then put down the cup and began, "At my grandfather's memorial service they didn't play hymns or the typical serious fare. No. They played one of Gumpy's favorite songs from the rock band *Queen*. The song was *Don't Stop Me Now*. I don't know if you've ever heard it, but the words go something like: *Don't stop me now because I'm having such a good time....* Well, that was Gumpy in a nutshell. He loved life and he had a good time living it—right up to the point when he lost Grandma. He was a true character; *a rocket out of control,* like the song says."

"Who made the decision to play that song at his service?"

"I don't know. Someone at the retirement village, I guess. He probably left instructions. It's the kind of thing Gumpy would do. I remember him as a man with a million interests and hobbies, and he was still riding a four-wheeler through the woods in his seventies. Gumpy was a fisherman, a writer, a college professor, and a horse breeder. After he retired, he started raising donkeys. He called his operation *Mich-Mash Donkey Farm—Donkeys of Distinction.* He had a sign in the front lawn. Years later, after he sold the donkeys, he changed the wording on the sign from 'Distinction' to 'Extinction.' When people asked where the donkeys were, he would tell them the donkeys went extinct. Global warming, he said, killed them—they couldn't tolerate the heat."

"No disrespect, but your grandfather sounds a little weird."

"Yes, I guess he was. He had the donkeys late in life. When he and grandma were younger they raised horses. They actually raced them for a while—Standardbred horses—trotters and pacers. Even though he was a professor, my grandparents preferred to live in the country, and he had a pretty big place – about 30 acres. It wasn't a farm exactly, more like a mini-farm or a country estate. We called their house *The Bottle House* because the tops of all their windows were lined with old, antique bottles from the nineteenth century. My grandparents dug them up from where an old outhouse and dump had once stood. They didn't have a garbage pickup service in the old days and people had to throw their trash and empty bottles somewhere. Gumpy and Grandma discovered a big hole on their property when they went hunting for old coins with a metal detector. They found lots of stuff in that hole, some coins, bottles, and old utensils and tools."

"Seriously?" Jessica asked. "They dug around in poop?"

Josh smiled and nodded. "Yeah, I guess they did. Gumpy and Grandma also had lots of birds. Their birds wandered everywhere: peacocks, ducks, and Guinea hens. I asked Gumpy once why he had so many birds and small animals. He said it was because they kept him connected to nature. He believed it was important not to forget one's place in the grand scheme of things."

"Nature again. I hate nature," Jessica said.

"I know, Jess. You told me that a few days ago."

"I don't know why your grandparents would want to surround themselves with dirty, filthy birds, and poke around poop in outhouses. They sound to me like they were pretty strange people."

"Not strange—wonderful! And it wasn't poop, not after a hundred-and-fifty years. It was soil, plain ordinary dirt. I know you probably can't understand this, but to them raising birds and horses and digging for old bottles was an adventure."

"You call that an adventure? Digging in crap? I wouldn't do that even if people had been throwing diamonds there instead of bottles."

"What if it was beauty products? You would dig for those, wouldn't you Jess? Say, for instance, it was an assortment of expensive make-up and hair care products— *Clinique, Ralph Lauren, Dior.* I bet you would be interested then. You'd probably start digging like a groundhog on steroids." Josh chuckled as he imagined Jessica on her knees pawing through the muck, grabbing glitzy bottles of makeup and perfume.

"That's not funny, Josh. You're being mean and obnoxious."

But Josh couldn't stop laughing. "I'm sorry, but it really is funny."

Jessica rose to her feet and grabbed her pocketbook. "Call me when your brother gets here and you get yourself under control. Remember, I want to be here when you open the box." She slammed the door as she left.

Josh noticed the rain had stopped.

Chapter 5

THE CONTENTS

Erik arrived at Josh's house two hours later. He came with his wife, Helen, and his two children, Harry and Olivia.

"Sorry I couldn't get here sooner," Erik said. "Mom and Dad told me to leave early, but the traffic was so bad coming through Miami that it didn't make any difference. I can't believe another box came! I mean, how is that even possible? Mom and Dad are curious, too. They want us to call them as soon as we open it."

"Now that you're here," Josh said, "I have to call Jessica. She was here earlier, and saw the box. She wants to be here when we open it, and I promised to call her when you arrived."

"Oh Josh… do you have to?"

"Yes, Erik. She is my fiancée, after all."

"Can we watch television, Uncle Josh? Mom said I had to ask permission."

"Of course you can." Josh bent and kissed the top of Olivia's head. "You and Harry can go in the den and watch whatever you like. Your box of toys is behind the couch."

"Say thank you to Uncle Josh," Helen said, "and *then* you can watch TV."

The little ones thanked their uncle and scampered off to the media room.

While Josh called Jessica, Erik examined the box on the table. He picked it up and shook it gently. Then he looked at the address label and smiled. Erik was a pleasant-looking man, with an open, congenial manner. He could converse with anyone, and made friends with everybody. He was of average height, with a solid, muscular build. The athlete of the family, he had a bookcase full of awards and trophies. Josh was the quieter brother, with a serious and contemplative nature. He spent his childhood taking things apart or breaking them so he could figure out how to put them back together again. Even as a young boy, when asked what he was interested in, Josh would reply, "Math and science." He never answered that he was interested in baseball or soccer, like his older brothers. Kevin, the oldest of the three, was an intellectual who enjoyed his career as a university professor. He loved to teach, write articles, and conduct research.

Although Erik looked like a weight-lifter, he had majored in business at college. While pursuing his degree he worked at the family nursery, and continued there after he graduated. He enjoyed the nursery because he was able to use both his business skills and his physical abilities. He liked the mix of indoor and outdoor work, and the demands of lifting and planting. Under his guidance the small business his uncles had started twenty years ago thrived and expanded. Thanks to Erik's marketing and business skills, *Victoria's Secret Garden Center* now easily supported four families. Erik couldn't be happier; he was doing exactly what he loved.

"Did you notice the return address?" Erik asked, when Josh returned from his call to Jessica. "It says *501 Celestial Drive,* and gives the name of the town as *Heaven*—no zip code."

"Yes, I saw that," Josh said. "It was the

first thing I noticed. It sounds like something Gumpy would do."

"But how? The only thing I can figure is that Gumpy must have been in cahoots with somebody. I don't believe they have UPS in heaven. I guess we could ask Mom. If anyone would know about heaven it's her." Erik was being sarcastic and referencing his mother's religiosity.

The doorbell rang and it was Jessica.

"Hi, Erik," she said, removing her jacket. "Nice to see you again." She kissed him lightly on his cheek. Then, she noticed his wife. "Oh Helen, you're here too? How good to see you." She opened her arms and gave Helen an awkward embrace. "Where are the children?"

"They're in the other room watching television."

"Well," Jessica said, "this is certainly a mystery, isn't it? Josh told me all about your Gumpy and his Adventure Boxes." She tossed her head back. "It's exciting! Do you want to hear an incredible story, something, like, really strange?" She didn't wait for an answer but lunched immediately into her story. "My friend Brenda... well Brenda likes to buy things. I like to buy things too, but I prefer to buy from regular stores, and I'm a lot more interested in fashion. Brenda buys a lot of stuff from eBay. Well, two weeks ago she bought this huge lot of vintage jewelry. Her mother has a booth in the antique mall and Brenda figures she can piece out some of the stuff and sell it in her mother's booth and make a little money. So she pays $20 and gets a shoebox full of old jewelry. Most of it is junk, stuff I certainly wouldn't want, but there's lots of it. So a few nights later Brenda is untangling the jewelry and separating the pieces. She notices that some pieces have little marks on the inside stamped on the metal, and she thinks they might be made of gold. Now, I love Brenda, you understand, but she is not the brightest bulb on the string, if you get my drift.

"So I'm skeptical when she tells me this story. But anyway, she puts a wedding band and two bracelets into a Ziploc bag and takes them to a jeweler, hoping she might be able to recover her twenty dollars. Anything she gets beyond that is profit. The jeweler examines the stuff and offers her six hundred dollars! Can you imagine? Of course Brenda takes the money. She runs back home and gives the contents a more careful examination.

She finds some earrings, tiny gold dots. So she takes these back to the jeweler, and gets another seventy-five dollars.

"When she told me, I couldn't believe it. I mean, I was so jealous! Stuff like that never happens to me. Well, okay, what's my point...? I'm thinking, like, maybe this box you got might contain something valuable, too."

Erik studied Jessica. She was wearing tight-fitting blue jeans, a red blouse, and spiked heels. Inch-long, gold earrings dangled and matched her gold necklace which consisted of several strands of chain. She told her story with such excitement and so many gesticulations he thought he was watching a theatrical performance. With her long blond hair and her sensational ensemble, Erik could never imagine Jessica buying anything from eBay. If it didn't have a designer label, Jessica wouldn't be interested. Josh had been dating Jessica for more than two years, but Erik still could be jolted by her appearance. He was amazed she and Josh were still together because they seemed so mismatched. Jessica always appeared to have just stepped out of a fashion magazine, while Josh walked around with his head in the clouds musing about nature, third-world poverty, and the greenhouse effect. No matter how hard he tried, Erik could not envision Jessica and his brother having a future together, but for the sake of Josh, he tried to hide his misgivings. It wasn't easy. Returning to reality, Erik said, "I've been thinking about the mystery all afternoon."

"Me too," Josh replied. "It was practically impossible to study."

They gathered around the table and from the breakfront drawer Josh pulled out some scissors. Then he cut the tape and ripped the box open. As he did he said "The box has practically no weight. It feels empty, but there must be something inside this Adventure Box."

Erik replied "I wouldn't be so certain. Remember, you're talking about Gumpy. Who knows what kind of adventure he planned for us this time?"

The first item removed from the box was a peacock feather. It was about eight inches long—a small eye feather. Josh removed the feather and held it up so everyone could see. He handed it to Erik, and Erik passed it to Helen. She took it, examined it, and offered it to Jessica.

Jessica shook her head no. "I'm not touching that thing, not without rubber gloves or sanitary wipes. It probably has germs and could make you sick."

Josh took the feather without answering Jessica, and laid it on the table. He reached in the box and removed a pocket watch on a chain. When he opened the watch, the inside of the cover held a tiny photograph of his grandparents.

"Look," he said. "How young they are!" He passed the watch to Erik, who looked and then passed it to Helen.

"I want to see," Jessica said. "It looks like an antique. It could be gold."

Helen held out the watch to Jessica. "Be careful," she said sarcastically. "Who knows where it's been? Maybe it's been up someone's ass like in the movie, *Pulp Fiction*."

Jessica reconsidered and withdrew her hand. "It's all right. I can see it from here," she said.

Helen and Erik exchanged amused glances. "There's one more thing," Josh said. He removed a folded sheet of ruled paper, the kind he used to do his homework on in grammar school. As Josh unfolded the paper it was clear there was some sort of crudely drawn diagram.

"What's that?" Erik asked.

"I'm not sure," Josh said, "but I think it's a map."

"A map to where?"

"I haven't the slightest idea. There are no words on it."

Both brothers quietly studied the paper, then Eric asked Josh for a magnifying glass. "It's kind of smudged or faded. I think it has a coffee stain."

Josh left the room and then shortly returned with the requested magnifier.

Erik bent over the paper, then straightened up to share his conclusion. "We have a map," he stated. "Let the adventure begin."

***

"That was disappointing," Jessica remarked. "You could have gotten this stuff at a yard sale. Of course, the watch might have some value. I'd take it to a jeweler and have it appraised."

No one responded to Jessica's assessment, and the silence was growing uncomfortable. "Well," she said, tossing her hair back,

"It's been fun, but I've got to run—a hair appointment." Jessica kissed Josh on the way out, and once she was gone the three remaining at the table sighed in collective relief.

Josh shrugged. "She means well, but I guess she was expecting more; something a little more sparkly."

"You mean like pirate gold?" Helen quipped.

Josh smiled. "That's my Jess; she always goes for the big show. It's her way. It's best to ignore some of the things she says."

"It isn't even *her* box. If there was a treasure, it wouldn't be hers under any circumstances," Erik said. "But who cares? I'm more curious about what this all means. What's really going on with this Adventure Box? Why did Gumpy go to all this trouble?"

"He didn't. He's gone," Josh said. "Someone did it for him."

"Okay, but who was his accomplice?"

"That's the mystery," Josh replied. "Maybe if I check with UPS I can find out who that someone is. UPS must have records. I'm sure they can find the name and address of the person who sent this box."

"Adventure Box," Erik said. "Remember,

it's not just any box, it's an Adventure Box. A certain degree of reverence needs to be displayed. It was sent to us by our Gumpy, not to Jessica, nor anyone else, to us—you and me!"

"I'm sorry, Erik, but I didn't think to exclude her. She's practically family, and she got so excited when I told her about the box. She's just Jessica being Jessica. After a while you get used to it."

"Whatever," Erik responded.

"Look," Josh said. "As soon as my test is done, I'll check with UPS and see if I can get to the bottom of this. I'll let you know as soon as I learn something."

"Thanks," Erik said. "I appreciate your efforts."

Jim & Cheryl Pahz

Chapter 6

ABBY

Josh called his brother the following week. "Erik, the Adventure Box came from Michigan; it was sent from Alma."

"Well, I'm not surprised. I knew there was a Hell, Michigan, so it makes sense there'd be a Heaven. You are aware Alma is where the Rose Retirement Village is located? Weren't you supposed to have visited Gumpy there before he died? And didn't you cancel your trip because of your girlfriend?"

"Yes, Erik. She had something important to do."

"Like what?"

"A beauty pageant."

"You cancelled your trip to see Gumpy, so you could take Jessica to a beauty pageant?"

"She was a contestant."

"Did she at least win?"

"No, she was runner-up."

"Jesus Christ, Josh! What a waste!"

"I know. Believe me, I feel terrible. Every time I think about it I want to cry. But I didn't know that would be my last chance to see him, and neither did you. But you know Jess, she's hard to refuse, and I owe her and her father an awful lot. I was just trying to keep her happy. If I could do it all over, I'd do things differently, but I can't change the past. I wish you'd stop criticizing me. I didn't visit Gumpy, but neither did you. You could have gone yourself, you know. But you're always too busy."

"You're right. I'm sorry," Erik apologized. "I don't mean to be so critical."

"I know," Josh said. "It's all right. Tomorrow I'll call the retirement village and see what I can find out."

"Sounds good. Keep me posted."

"I will, Erik."

"How did you do on your exam?"

"I passed. I'm still a student. I haven't failed out yet."

"You won't fail out. You're too smart. Science and math, remember? Let me know anything you find out."

"You know I will, Erik."

***

"I'm sorry." The faceless voice on the telephone responded. "I don't know anything about it. I can ask some of the staff, but I doubt I'll find the information you're looking for. I remember your grandfather, of course. He was a sweet man, but he's been gone for more than a year. A lot happens in a year around here, a lot of changes."

"Anything you could do would be appreciated," Josh said. "It would mean a lot to me and my family."

"I'll do my best," the woman responded. "I promise."

"May I ask your name?" Josh inquired.

"Mrs. Butterworth," the woman answered. "Like the syrup. I am Amanda Butterworth, but I only work part time. I'm here on Tuesdays, Thursdays, and Saturdays."

"How about I wait a week and call you next Tuesday?" Josh asked. "Is that convenient?"

"Certainly, young man."

"Thank you so much, Mrs. Butterworth. I appreciate your help."

"You're very welcome."

It was hard, but Josh was able to wait a full week before calling Mrs. Butterworth back. When he got her on the phone, she was excited to report what she had found out.

"Here's what I learned," she said. "Your grandfather was attended to by several of our staff, but by one person in particular—a young woman named Abigail. I heard she read a lot of poetry to him. Abigail has worked here about five years; she's a lovely person. If anyone would know about your grandfather, it would be her. If you want, I can check to see if she would be willing to speak with you. I'd have to check with her first, of course—it's policy. If she's agreeable I can give you her phone number."

"Yes! Great. That would be wonderful," Josh said. "Thank you for all your help."

"There is one thing I would like to ask you. After you grandfather's funeral some of his personal effects were picked up by a daughter, and the rest of his belongings were shipped to family in Florida. It was all according to the instructions he left. Was something out of order or missing? Is there some irregularity we need to know about?"

"Oh no," Josh said, "nothing like that.

My concern is of a personal nature. There's nothing to be alarmed about."

"Oh good," Mrs. Butterworth said. "I always worry. I am one of those people who worry about everything."

A short time later Mrs. Butterworth called back with the information for Josh. The woman's full name was Abigail Murphy. Josh looked at the phone number he had written down, and tried to compose his thoughts. What would he say to Ms. Murphy without sounding crazy? And there was so much more he wanted to know. What were Gumpy's last days like? What kind of poetry did she read to him? The longer Josh thought about it, the more certain he became. He decided not to call Abigail Murphy. *This shouldn't be done over the telephone,* he thought, *I need to meet the woman who cared for my Gumpy. I want to talk with her face-to-face.* Josh folded the piece of paper with the telephone number and slipped it in his wallet. Then he dialed up Erik.

"I got the name and number of the woman who cared for Gumpy, but I don't want to do this over the phone. I'd like to go to Michigan and meet with her. Can you come with me?"

"Not now, Josh. I can't get away. It's the

busiest time of the year for us. How about in a couple of months? Can you wait until spring?"

"Sure, Erik, I can wait. I need to concentrate on school anyway. I can't really get away until the end of the semester."

"Couldn't Kevin meet this woman?"

"No. Don't you remember? He's in Guatemala on sabbatical, working for the Pan American Health Organization."

"Right. I forgot. When is he coming home?"

"Not till the end of summer. Late August, I think, or September."

"Okay. Then we'll plan to go when the semester's done. Say Josh, I think I figured out Gumpy's map."

"Really? Tell me."

"I think it's a map of Gumpy's driveway— his old place, before he and Grandma moved to the retirement village."

"Why do you think that?"

"It's the two black circles. I think those are the two big rocks on either side of the driveway."

"That makes sense, but what's in the spot with the X? Where is Gumpy leading us?"

"I'm not sure, Josh. I think ...." Erik

hesitated, and then he continued "It could be those swords."

"The swords? You mean the legendary swords? The ones that were, but never were?"

"Those be them."

"Well, if so, we'll probably dig them up."

"Should we? I mean, what about the curse?"

"Erik, you don't really believe that nonsense! That was just a silly tale we were told as children. Gumpy was pulling our leg. Besides, I'm a man of science. I don't believe in fairy tales, or goblins, or curses."

"Okay, Josh, I just thought… I suppose you're right. But you might think twice before opening up that can of worms."

***

Summer came and the semester was over. Josh approached Erik about the trip to Michigan, but there always seemed to be a conflict with Erik's schedule. Finally Josh decided to simply pick a date and go—with or without Erik.

In the end, Erik couldn't make the trip. "It's all right," Josh said. "Don't worry. It'll be fine."

"Why not stay at Kevin's place? I'm sure Natalie would put you up, and you could spend some time with the kids."

"Maybe I'll do that. Mount Pleasant is only about twenty minutes from Alma. Maybe Natalie will put me up for a few days. It would be nice to see the boys again."

"Of course. And I'm sure they'd love a visit from their Uncle Josh."

"I'll give Natalie a call and ask her if it will be all right."

***

Josh got to Michigan in July, and it felt good to escape the heat of southern Florida. Kevin's house was located in a neighborhood referred to as *Pill Hill*, because so many doctors lived there. Kevin and Natalie had purchased their ranch home on Greenbanks Drive four years ago, and it was easy to see why. The area was lovely with lush green lawns and beautiful older homes. The neighborhood had a pastoral quality, but was actually convenient to all the amenities of town. In good weather Kevin walked to the university where he taught.

Natalie looked the same as the last time Josh saw her. She was a petite woman with short, brown hair cut in a bob. Josh usually didn't care for short hair on a woman, but it looked good on Natalie. The children had grown considerably since Josh last saw them. Alex was now five years of age and his older brother, Zachary, was seven. Both boys were exuberant and couldn't wait to show Uncle Josh all of their toys.

"We got a Wii, Uncle Josh! Can you play it with us?"

"Sure," Josh replied. "I'd love to." And he meant it. Now that he was actually in Michigan he knew he'd made the right decision in coming. And he felt an outpouring of affection for his nephews.

After playing video games with the children for what seemed like forever, Josh took a break and had coffee with Natalie.

"So," Josh said. "What is the latest from Kevin?"

"He's very happy living in Guatemala and working on a nutrition program—something to do with soybeans. The soybean meal is turned into chicken feed. They have a big poultry industry in Guatemala. *Pollo Camparo*, the chicken franchise, goes through a lot of chickens. They have those restaurants all over the country."

"I remember," Josh said. "It's the best

tasting chicken I've ever eaten. Do you know they recently franchised *Pollo Camparo* in Florida. I think *KFC* is going to have some real competition."

"Kevin's project is not about chicken feed. It has something to do with nutritional deficiency for the indigenous population. Apparently soybean meal has a high nutritional value and it's being introduced into other food products. I don't know exactly what it's about. I just know Kevin is enjoying his sabbatical and feels like he's participating in something worthwhile. As far as I'm concerned, I just want the time to pass quickly, because I want him home, and so do the children."

"He'll be back soon," Josh said. "The time will go by quickly."

The following day, Josh drove to the Rose Retirement Village. The driveway was about one quarter mile long and circled a well manicured green lawn that was dotted with several specimen trees. The circle ended in front of a large, impressive building that looked more like a small castle than a home for seniors. Although fairly new, the Rose Retirement Village was designed to look like it could be over a hundred years old. There was a rose garden and patio area on the south side of the building, and Josh admired a profusion of roses in bloom as he walked to the entrance. Once inside, Josh followed the signs to the Visitor Services Office. He asked for Ms. Abigail Murphy, and was instructed to wait in the reception area. He sat on a couch and admired the elegant surroundings. The beauty inside matched the splendor of the outside. The room was spacious, with tile floors on which were laid Persian carpets. The walls contained many works of art, mainly pictures of flowers.

A young woman in a starched nurse's uniform approached him. She was about five feet, six inches tall, neither fat nor thin. Her auburn hair was pulled back in bun, and she wore wire-rimmed glasses.

Although she had a business-like demeanor, she offered a winsome smile when she saw Josh. She extended her hand. "Hello. I am Abby Murphy. Do you like our paintings? Most were done by our residents. If you look carefully, you might notice that the rose in all its forms is the primary subject. Can I be of assistance to you?"

"I am Joshua Lagos-Ross, the grandson of Daniel Ross. He lived here for a couple of years before he died."

"Yes, of course. I remember your grandfather well. He was one of those people who stays in your heart."

"Excuse me; I'm not sure I understand your meaning."

"It's like this—in my profession, I see many people. Most are nameless faces who enter your life and then pass through it. You forget them almost as soon as they leave. Then there are the few, and I emphasize the word few, who you really get to know personally and who become close friends. It doesn't happen often, but once in a while...." The woman paused and then smiled again. "Your grandfather was one of those people. He stuck in my heart."

"I heard something similar from my brother, Kevin. Only he wasn't talking about patients; he was talking about students. He teaches at the university in Mount Pleasant. He said once in a while a student comes along and becomes a friend. All the others just pass by and you forget them as soon as they leave."

"Your brother teaches at Central Michigan University?"

"Yes, but not now. He's on sabbatical

and living in Guatemala. He's working with the Pan American Health Organization. I'm staying temporarily at his house with his family."

"How nice. Tell me, Josh, what can I do for you?"

"If it's not too great an imposition, I'd like to hear about my grandparents. Whatever you might remember no matter how insignificant it might seem. They were very important to me and my brothers. I wasn't here at the end, and I'd just like to know about their final days and their life here. I want to find and preserve as many memories as possible. I'm also trying to solve a mystery and I think, by talking with you, I might solve it more quickly."

Abby had a kind and concerned face, and Josh imagined she must have been a comfort to his grandfather. "I understand, and I am happy to help in whatever way I can. I didn't know your grandmother well, but I did get to spend a lot of time with your grandfather after she passed away. I was one of his nurses, but it was more than that. I like to believe we became friends. I spent a lot of time with him; he liked to be read to—especially poetry."

"I heard," Josh said, "Mrs. Butterworth told me."

"Unfortunately, you caught me at a bad time. I'm working now and will be on call for several more hours. Maybe we could meet again when I'm free? Would tomorrow afternoon be all right? I'm off duty tomorrow."

"Sure," Josh answered. "Tomorrow is fine. What would be a good time?"

"How about we meet at four in the afternoon?"

Josh nodded. "No problem. Where should we meet?"

"I live in Mount Pleasant, too. Since that is where you're staying, how about we meet in the lobby of the university library?"

"Okay. I'll see you tomorrow at 4:00."

Chapter 7

FINGERS IN THE SKY

Josh arrived at the library fifteen minutes early the next afternoon. He was anxious to see Abby again, and a little nervous. *What's wrong with me?* He wondered. *This is silly.* He decided to wait outside because the afternoon was so lovely. The temperature was perfect with just a whisper of a breeze. He'd never seen such a blue sky, which served as a bold backdrop for the wispy white clouds.

He noticed Abby walking toward the library before she saw him, and he took the opportunity to fully assess her as she approached the entrance. Although she was not a small woman, there was a delicate, refined quality about her. Today her hair hung loose to just below her shoulders. She was without her glasses or other adornments and Josh was struck by the elegance of her features. The phrase *easy on the eyes* came to him, as his eyes drank in Abby's uncomplicated natural beauty. Jessica was beautiful, too, he reminded himself, but in an entirely different way: a loud, raw, scream-in-your-face way. Abby's beauty was subtle, like a painting done in pastels. He found it refreshing.

Suddenly Abby glanced up and saw Josh looking at her. He felt himself blush, but she seemed not to notice. She smiled broadly in recognition and waved. He smiled back and walked down the steps to join her. Because of the comfortable temperature they decided to take a walk around campus. Abby knew a place close by where they could get an ice cream or shake. As they walked to the soda shop Josh tried to keep up his end of the conversation, but found himself distracted by his companion. Abby looked younger today, and innocent. She wore faded jeans and a white tee shirt. She had a poppy-colored tote slung over her shoulder and Josh could see the top of a rolled-up *People Magazine* sticking out. To observers she was just another coed walking on campus. But to Josh there was nothing ordinary about the smoothness of her skin or the way that the breeze tugged at her hair.

"Look at that sky," Abby said, pointing upward.

Josh looked up at the startling blueness. The air smelled fresh with just a hint of lavender—was it from a garden or from Abby's perfume? Then he noticed the white clouds that streaked diagonally across the sky. "The clouds look like fingers," Josh said. "Strange."

"Like a hand, as if they're the fingers of God."

"Yes," Josh replied. "It's amazing. Maybe it's a clue."

"Nature is so spectacular," said Abby.

Josh nodded in agreement. Then something clicked in his head, and he realized that Abby reminded him of his grandfather. It wasn't her appearance, of course, but her sense of wonder and the way she strung words together. She seemed comfortable with herself and the world, the same way Gumpy did. Josh wondered if that was why he was so preoccupied with her. "That's exactly what my grandfather would have said if he'd have seen those clouds."

Abby smiled. "I spent a lot of time with him. He had a genuine reverence for nature and everything wild. I once asked him if he wanted to watch the news on television, and he said no. The news, he told me, caused him to despair. Then he asked me to find a nature program for him, which I did. Your grandfather talked a lot about the past—like riding the four-wheelers in the woods with you and your brothers, and all the times you fished together. He talked about your grandmother, too; he missed her terribly. After she passed away, you boys were the light of his life. He was so proud of you."

"I know," Josh said. Suddenly he felt the weight of regret for not visiting Gumpy when he had the chance. "I was supposed to visit him shortly before he died, but…."

Abby softly filled the pause, "I'm sure you had a good reason, and I'm sure your grandfather understood."

Right, Josh thought, *a beauty pageant, a stupid beauty pageant—meaningless, a waste of time.* He was too ashamed to confess this to Abby.

"What did you mean by *a clue?*" Abby asked. "You know, the fingers in the sky?"

"It was an idea my grandfather had. He

used to say that God left clues for us to find. He said God scattered them like Easter eggs and if we had our eyes open we would discover them. The more we found, the better life would be. Gumpy believed we are all part of nature. 'Never forget that,' he said. 'If you lose your connection to nature, you will surely lose your way, like a man without a compass.' Then he told me to look at the peacock. He'd say: 'See those colors, that pattern on his tail feathers? God has left a clue. Always keep your eyes open to the wonders of nature; that's where you'll find God.'"

They had reached the soda shop and decided to go inside. It was fairly empty so they had their pick of tables. They decided on one at the front window where they could catch some afternoon sun. Abby ordered a chocolate shake with lots of whipped cream on top and Josh got an Arctic Swirl. Between ordering and sipping their drinks, the conversation about Gumpy continued to flow.

"Was your grandfather a religious man?"

"Yes, but not in the traditional sense. Certainly not like my mom and dad; they're always in church. But Gumpy was different.

I guess you could call him ecclesiophobic."

"What's that?"

"Someone who fears churches. Actually, that's not correct. He wasn't afraid of churches; he just didn't like attending them. He and Grandma were spiritual, but not really religious. They valued all forms of life, not just human.

"I remember one winter here in Michigan when I was a kid helping my grandpa with his peacocks. Most of the year the birds were permitted to wander freely around the farm, but in winter Gumpy and Grandma locked them up in a shed. You see, peacocks like to roost in trees, and if they're left outside during the winter their feet will freeze to the tree branches. Then they'll be stuck in the trees and die.

"So every November, before Thanksgiving, the peacocks and whatever other birds were there would be lured into the bird house and locked up till spring. Usually the whole process took about a week, but this one year two stubborn peacocks refused to go in. Each day they got a little hungrier and colder and they knew all the other birds were inside, but they didn't want to give up their freedom.

"Grandma stopped feeding them except for each evening when she'd open the door and put food and water on the floor inside the shed to tempt them. Of course we knew that eventually they'd get hungry enough to walk inside, but they were taking so long that Gumpy was afraid a storm would get them first. After a week of disappointing attempts, Gumpy shook his head and said, 'I don't know, Josh, we might lose these two birds. They're smart enough to know we want to lock them inside with the other birds. Even though they're hungry they know not to go after the corn in there if they want to remain free. This is like a game to them. Unfortunately, what they don't know is that I'm trying to save their lives, and if they don't get inside soon they'll be finished. They will surely die.' We stood watching the two birds and considering their fate. An ice storm was due to arrive in two days. Then Gumpy got philosophical and said he thought the bird situation was similar to how it is between God and man. God tries to help us and guide us toward safety. He leaves clues and puts up roadblocks to help steer us in the right direction. But just like those stubborn peacocks, we ignore the obvious and are determined to have our own way. Gumpy said, 'We can no more fathom the mind of God than those peacocks can understand our intentions.'"

"Well?" Abby asked. She leaned forward, gripping her milkshake as she anxiously searched his face.

"What?" Josh was confused.

"What about the peacocks, for heaven's sake? Did they ever get locked up?"

"Oh! Yeah," he said and smiled. "Actually they both walked in the next afternoon, all casual and nonchalant as if they'd planned it all along. They made it just in time because the following day we had a giant snowstorm. They really would have died if they'd have stayed outside."

"I see what you mean about your grandparents being spiritual," Abby said.

"They loved nature; I think nature was their theophany. And they didn't approve of us playing video games or spending too much time in front of the television. Gumpy said it was a waste of time and you only had so much time allotted to you. It's a hard concept for a kid to understand. 'When it's gone,' Gumpy said, 'it's gone, and you can't get it back. Remember,' he said, 'every day is a gift. Besides, too much TV or time spent playing video games will turn your brains into Jell-O. Then you'll be like those peacocks, but not as good looking.'"

Abby smiled. Josh noticed she was almost done with her shake, and he realized he didn't want the afternoon to end. He liked talking to Abby. In fact he couldn't remember having talked so much about himself in a long time. With Jessica he did most of the listening—to her or to his music. Maybe it was because Jessica already knew his stories, or maybe it was because she just wasn't interested in what he had to say. For whatever reason it seemed like ages since he'd talked so much about things that were important to him, and he didn't want to stop. He felt a twinge of guilt as if he were somehow betraying Jessica.

"I'm jealous, Josh. When I hear you talk about your grandparents and their birds and four-wheelers it sounds like you had a stereotypically perfect childhood."

Josh shook his head. "Not quite," he said. "There's nothing stereotypical about my family. My grandparents never had biological children, so they decided to adopt. When that didn't go as quickly as they wanted, they traveled to Central America and worked out the details themselves. That's when they adopted my Aunt Ahsley. Then they went a step further and started their own adoption agency so they could help others."

"I thought your grandfather taught at the university."

"He did, but he also was the director for the agency. Basically Grandma did most of the paperwork for the courts and immigration and manned the agency while Gumpy did the foreign travel and made contacts with churches and orphanages. That's how he met my mom. She was just a young girl, working in the home of a family in Guatemala. Gumpy had hired the man's wife to translate agency documents. One day when he was visiting their house he met my mother. She was 13 years old at the time. Gumpy slipped her five quetzales when no one was looking. Quetzales are the currency of Guatemala, like our dollars. It was a little gift. Anyway, on subsequent visits he came to know her and was impressed with her quick wit and abilities, so he and Grandma decided to try to help her to get into the U.S. That way, they figured, she could get an education. After speaking with various judges and officials they found out the only way to get Mom to the U.S. was if they adopted her. So that's what they did. She was fifteen years old when they brought her home."

"That is quite a story," Abby said. "I had no idea. Your grandparents certainly lived a full life. What about your mom? It must have been quite an adjustment for her as a teenager."

"From what I've been told it was rough for a while, but they worked it out. My mother learned to speak English, and graduated from high school. She was visiting family back in Guatemala when she met my dad and got married. Later my parents returned to Michigan, bought a house, and started their family. My mom's brothers from Guatemala all came to the United States and settled in Florida. They opened a nursery business. About seventeen years ago my parents moved to Florida and went into business with her brothers.

"Moving to Florida was hard for Erik and me. Gumpy was in my life from the day I was born until the day we moved. He was at the hospital when Mom delivered me. Mom asked him to get her something to eat from the cafeteria and, because I was somewhat of a hairy baby, Gumpy suggested getting a banana for me. My dad has never completely forgiven Gumpy for that insensitive remark. But Gumpy was joking and my dad didn't have much of a sense of humor and his English was poor. Gumpy was just trying to be funny.

"One of the things I missed most about Michigan was going trick-or-treating with Gumpy. He loved Halloween and bought us our costumes. Then he drove us to what he considered the best neighborhoods for candy and treats. After we moved to Florida, we stopped going out on Halloween. We were getting older by then, and there was more crime in Florida, but the main reason we stopped trick-or-treating was because the church discouraged the practice. My mom and dad are still religious. They go to church every Sunday morning and Wednesday night."

"How did your parents get along with Gumpy? Was religion a problem?"

"You mean Gumpy's ideas about God and clues in nature?"

Abby nodded.

"Well, they definitely thought my grandparents should go to church. They didn't talk much about the other stuff. As Gumpy would say, they agreed to disagree."

"I think Gumpy was right, Josh, about the clues God leaves to keep us on the right path. I've often thought that beetles are a clue to something."

"The rock group?"

"No, silly. Beetles, real beetles. The insects. Have you ever noticed how some are so beautifully colored – incandescent really? Chrysomelidea and Burprestidae come to mind. The backs of those beetles have the most beautiful iridescent colors. I believe those are clues also."

Who is this girl? Josh thought. *She actually knows the names of bugs. This is extraordinary!*

"You really should check them out sometime," Abby said. "I think you'll be surprised. It's almost as if nature is the language of God—His way of writing a poem. I imagine He must be pleased when we appreciate His efforts."

"Abby, you just reminded me of something I haven't thought of in years." Josh leaned back in his chair and his face had the look of someone lost in a memory. "The Jehovah's Witnesses used to visit Gumpy every couple of months to talk about the Bible. My grandmother always hid in the bedroom when they came, but Gumpy actually looked forward to their visits. He loved to talk about the Bible. Anyway, they were always trying to get Gumpy to go to their church. Gumpy always declined the invitation. He told them he was in church every day. He said something like, 'Every time I am in the woods I am close to God.' The Witnesses didn't appreciate his theology. They would open their Bibles and read verses trying to convince Gumpy he was wrong. Then Gumpy would recite this one poem by Emily Dickenson."

"What was the poem?" Abby asked.

"I don't know. It's been a long time. I can't remember it except that it had something to do with a bobolink. I'll have to look it up. Maybe I'll have the name of it the next time I see you."

"That would be great. I look forward to it."

"You've been awfully kind, Abby, to listen to me go on and on about Gumpy. I can't remember when I've talked so much. I'm usually the quiet one. I invited you here so you could tell me about Gumpy, and here

I am babbling away."

Abby reached across the table and took Josh's hand. "I like listening to you, Josh. It's hard to describe, but I find it fulfilling to actually meet one of the boys your grandfather spent so much time talking to me about. When I hear your stories it's like I'm visiting with Daniel again. I never knew my grandparents. They died when I was very young. When I try to imagine my grandfather, Gumpy pops up in my mind. Thank you so much for sharing your memories with me. What I can share with you is that when he died, your grandfather was content and at peace with his life. After your grandmother had passed, and after his stroke, he told me he was ready. He said he had lived a full and satisfying life and he had no regrets. He was physically tired, like a child who had played hard all day and was ready for a good night's sleep. That was the way he put it. He wasn't looking forward to dying—he wasn't ready to telephone Dr. Kevorkian for assistance—but he wasn't fighting time either. He said he wanted to see your grandmother again, on the other side, as well as other relatives and friends who had passed away. But then he would chuckle and say something like, 'I hope there is another side.' He never lost his sense of humor. He had a healthy skepticism, but I believe he was a man of faith. He wasn't afraid to die."

"He wasn't in pain when…?" asked Josh hesitantly.

"No, Josh, I don't believe so. He passed during the night in his sleep. I had visited him earlier that day. I don't really remember anything specific he talked about, except that he asked me to move a vase closer to his bed so he could look at it. I remember because it wasn't your typical vase filled with flowers. The vase he wanted was full of peacock feathers. They were quite beautiful and he seemed to enjoy looking at them."

"Thank you," Josh said, "for being there for him."

Abby shrugged. "Your grandfather was special."

"Gumpy had a thing for peacock feathers. He said the best artist in the world could never conceive of anything so beautiful as the tail feathers of a peacock. Only the mind of God could create such a perfect work of art. Do you know, Abby, that when Mohammed ascended to paradise he did it on the back of a creature that supposedly had the face of a woman, the body of a mule, and the tail of a peacock? I think the animal's name was el-Buraq."

"You mean like the president's name?"

"Maybe, but I could be wrong about the name."

"Josh, how do you know this? Are you of the Muslim faith?"

"No, Abby. I'm a Baptist, just like Gumpy, and my mom and dad. I know this stuff because Gumpy told me. My head is filled with all sorts of useless information that I learned from my grandfather. I find it only helps me when I'm playing Trivial Pursuit, or talking with pretty women, like you. Gumpy knew all sorts of stuff. He was a pretty smart guy, well read and unbeatable at Scrabble."

"Well, Josh, if you're so smart, how do you explain the vulture? Is it one of God's masterpieces? It's an ugly bird and nasty, and it likes to chow-down on dead things."

Josh looked confused. He didn't know how to respond. "What?"

"A vulture. The bird that swoops down and feeds on the leftovers left by the lions." Then she paused and smiled, "I'm teasing, Josh." She touched his hand again and then pulled away. "Beauty is relative and who knows what's beautiful to God? He must have created everything for a purpose."

"I've never thought of that." Josh answered. "The vulture isn't a pretty image. But there's a lot I don't understand."

"I believe in clues too," Abby said. "But I don't think we're supposed to understand everything. Sometimes I think that being alive is like being on a stage. We're not supposed to know all that's happening behind the curtain. Our job is to be on the stage playing our parts and living our life as best we can. As far as vultures are concerned, I think your grandfather would have said vultures have their place, too. They are the sanitation workers, like snapping turtles."

"That's amazing! On the subject of snapping turtles," Josh exclaimed enthusiastically, "we had snapping turtles in Gumpy's pond! My brothers and I always wanted to trap and kill them, but Gumpy wouldn't let us. He said when fish die, the snapping turtles feed on their bodies and by doing so keep the pond clean and healthy. He told us we should have reverence for life— all life." Josh paused and looked directly into Abby's eyes. Her eyes were liquid brown, like melted chocolate. To Josh they were the most comforting he had ever seen.

"Abby, there was a peacock feather in the Adventure Box. I'll have to tell you about that. It is what brought me here."

Abby squeezed his hand and smiled. "Maybe your grandfather was sending you a clue."

Chapter 8

DORA

"Now you got it," the old man said. "We're almost there. Keep walking in this direction. I think I'm right."

"Thank you for helping me," Dora said. "I couldn't have found the way without you. I'm so confused." She looked at him and his facial features began to come into focus. Still, he was more of a shadow figure than a real person.

"You would find your way, with or without me. Alone, it just might take longer. But together we'll make it out of here. And it is much more pleasant, having company."

"Are we dead?"

"I'm not sure, but I don't think so. If we are, then the afterlife is nothing like I imagined."

"But if we're not dead, where are we?"

"That's a good question. Unfortunately, I don't have an answer. I've been wrestling with that one myself."

"Maybe we're in purgatory?"

"Maybe, but I'm Baptist. We don't believe in purgatory."

"That doesn't mean it doesn't exist. I think the greater probability is that I am asleep and dreaming. I am having an *Alice in Wonderland* type of experience. But I'm not Alice; my name is Dora. Do you know how long we've been walking together?"

"I'm not sure of that either. I think it's been a while. I've lost all sense of time, but am I in your dream or are you in mine? That is the question. Sometimes I hear words, poetry mostly, but then the words fade away. My name is Daniel. I'm sure of that much."

"As Alice said, in her visit to Wonderland, it just keeps getting *curiouser and curiouser*. I have a daughter," Dora said, "and a husband. They must be worried."

"Yes," the old man replied, "I imagine they are. Do you have any idea how you got here?"

"I'm not sure. It might have something to

do with a car accident."

"I see."

"What about you? How did you wind up here?"

"I've been trying to remember, but I can't. Like you, I'm confused. I opened my medicine cabinet and saw lots of lights—just like a football stadium at night. Then I was here. I know it sounds crazy."

They walked silently for a little distance. Then Dora said, "I don't hear words, but I keep hearing a noise that sounds like a duck."

"Sometimes I hear that too," Daniel said. "I'm not sure what it is. If it's a duck, it's not mine. I had ducks once, but that was a long time ago. I don't believe it's a real duck; it just sounds like one."

"Then what do you suppose it is?"

"I believe it's part of this reality ... this place ... but I don't think this reality is purgatory. I think the duck goes with the territory, like the whirring sound I also hear. Those sounds belong here—wherever *here* is."

"Are you hearing words now?" Dora asked.

"Yes, in the background. This is what I'm hearing:

There was a time when meadow,

grove and stream,

The earth, and every common sight, did seem,

Apparell'd in celestial light...."

"Isn't that Wordsworth?"

"Yes, I believe it is. It's nice. I like it."

"Me too. It's lovely. I wish I could hear poetry instead of that silly duck."

"I hear the duck, too. Try not to pay attention to it. I don't think it will hurt us. I once had donkeys. "

Chapter 9

A DATE

Josh's afternoon with Abby flew by much too fast, and there still seemed so much to say. He hadn't asked Abby about the Adventure Box! The two agreed to have dinner together on Saturday, and Josh vowed to himself that he would stay focused and talk to Abby about the mystery he had traveled to Michigan to solve. But the fact that he so enjoyed Abby's company caught him off guard. As he drove back to Natalie's house, Josh reprimanded himself. *I'm engaged to be married. I'm not in Michigan to meet women. Why am I thinking so much about Abby? What about Jessica?* But the problem was, he didn't want to think about Jessica. He was surprised to discover he didn't even miss Jessica. He hadn't thought about her since he arrived in Michigan. He decided he'd call her that night. Maybe hearing her voice would spark something. He should check his email, too, and make contact with Erik.

***

"Josh!" Jessica answered her phone. "Why haven't you answered my email? How are you?"

"I'm sorry, Jess," he said. "I haven't checked my emails yet. I'll have to wrangle the laptop away from the kids later. Is everything all right?"

"That's why you need a smart phone. You don't even text! How am I supposed to reach you?"

"Just call me, Jessica. That's what the cell phone is for. If I don't answer, you can call Natalie or leave a message."

"Well tell me what's going on. You know, I should be angry with you. Did you learn who sent the Adventure Box?"

"Not yet, but I'm working on it. I think I might have an answer in a couple of days. It's a little more complicated than I thought."

"I miss you, Josh. I'm bored. When are

you coming home?"

"In a week or so," Josh said. It was the first he had thought of returning to Florida, and he realized he wasn't ready to leave Michigan yet. There was nothing he immediately needed to return for, except, maybe Jessica.

Jessica wailed, "A week! What am I supposed to do while you're gone? Amber and Dave are having their housewarming party next weekend. You have to be back by then."

"I wouldn't count on it, Babe. I've got a lot of things to do," he lied.

"Like what?" From her voice he could tell she was pouting now. He imagined her sitting in the middle of her bed surrounded by her favorite fashion magazines. She probably had those big curlers in her hair in preparation for a night out with the girls.

"Meetings, you know, to find out about Gumpy and the Adventure Box. And some family stuff with my Aunt Ashley, and Natalie and the kids. I promised I'd take them to the water park. It's been a year since I've been here, so I'd like to spend a little time."

"Oh." Jessica didn't hide her disappointment.

"What about you? Tell me what you've been doing," Josh said to change the topic.

"Well, I went shopping with Daphne today. And tonight I'm meeting the girls at CoCo's—it's their girl's night. Oh, and Josh, I picked out some designs for our wedding invitations."

"What?" Josh hoped his voice didn't sound as shocked as he felt. He took a deep breath and continued, "Isn't that a bit premature? There's nothing definite yet, we haven't even set a date, Jess."

Jessica laughed, "Silly Josh. If I left things up to you we'd never get married. A wedding takes a lot of planning if you want to do it right. We've only got a year, so it's time to get started. But don't worry; I'll handle the details."

Suddenly Josh didn't feel so good. He had a sinking feeling in his stomach and he was beginning to perspire—the way he felt when he was pulled over by a police car, even when he was certain he had done nothing wrong.

"Do you miss me, honey?" Jessica's voice was now sweet and enticing.

"Yes, of course," Josh said, feeling slightly nauseous.

"I'm cooking up a surprise for you,"

Jessica said. "But I gotta go. So you just sit tight, okay? I'll see you soon."

"Okay, Jess. Bye."

"Bye Josh. I love you."

"Me, too," Josh said and hung up the phone in relief. He immediately headed for the shower. He needed to cool off and clear his head. He had to wash away his misgivings.

***

Josh spent Friday playing with his nephews and trying not to think about either Abby or Jessica. After breakfast they played video games. Lunch was burgers at McDonald's followed by an afternoon of fun at the Soaring Eagle Water Park. The three stopped for ice cream at Doozies and returned home to Natalie at 4:30. Josh was exhausted but the boys were still going strong. They rushed off to the family room for more video games. Natalie took one look at Josh and said, "You need a nap. Those munchkins are a lot to handle. Why don't you lie down until dinner?"

Josh gladly did as he was told and slept soundly until 6:00, when he awoke to see

Alex staring at him from the foot of the bed. Josh sat up and rubbed his eyes. "How long have you been there?" Josh asked.

Alex shrugged. Josh noticed Alex was holding Vincent, the black and white cat. Vincent was old, and lazy, and enormous— actually an armful for Alex. The cat stretched out lengthwise across Alex's arms and purred loudly as he looked up trustingly at the boy.

"What's up, buddy?" Josh asked.

"Mom said to come get you. Dinner's ready."

Josh followed Alex and Vincent to the dinner table. After dinner Josh played catch with the boys while Natalie cleaned the kitchen. Later, they all watched a video, and then had milk and cookies before bed. Josh was relieved to have gotten through the day and was tired enough that he didn't even care when he found Vincent asleep at the end of his bed. He kept the door open a bit so Vincent could leave whenever he was ready. Josh fell asleep to the sound of Vincent's purr.

The next morning Josh answered his emails while the boys watched cartoons. He hadn't used his computer since his arrival in Michigan. It felt good to catch up. Then he headed to Kohl's department store to buy a new shirt for his dinner with Abby. Although he could still find his way around, the town had significantly changed in the seventeen years since his family had moved. It seemed to have quadrupled in size, but everywhere he drove amidst the new shops and restaurants he would catch a glimpse of the older places that still held memories. The Kmart and Dollar Store were still there—favorite haunts of Gumpy when he took Josh and his brothers on shopping trips for toys and candy. Their favorite pet store was still in operation, as well as the Orange Julius place. Josh thought of Gumpy and his heart swelled. Josh had never wanted to leave Michigan when his parents moved to Florida. To him, Michigan had always been home. But where there had previously been empty pastures, now whole shopping centers appeared. He felt nostalgic as he made his way through familiar neighborhoods. Mount Pleasant still felt like home.

***

Finally it was time for Josh to pick Abby up for dinner. Her residence was easy for

Josh to find. Mount Pleasant was still a small town that stretched along a four-mile strip of highway known as Mission Street. At the south end was the new shopping center with big chain stores like Walmart and Kohl's. It seemed apartments were everywhere. Probably the new apartments were where students lived. In the old part of town many of the Victorian-style homes had "For Rent" signs in the windows. When he was younger those old houses rented rooms and were always full of students. Apparently, the students had migrated to the newer apartments. The university dominated the west side of Mission Street and was interspersed with pockets of older residential areas. On the east side was the Soaring Eagle Casino. This part of town was nourished by a new crop of franchise restaurants and motels.

Abby's house was a few miles from where Josh's brother, Kevin, lived. Kevin was on Greenbanks, just a couple of blocks from the university campus. Abby's house was on the east side of Mission Street in an older residential area between the high school and hospital. The houses in Abby's neighborhood were older and smaller, with tree-lined streets and sidewalks. They looked like they were built in the 1940s or 1950s. Many of the bungalow-style homes had a welcoming front porch surrounded by a garden. As it was midsummer, they were all at their height of beauty. Josh smiled in remembrance; this was one of Gumpy's favorite trick-or-treat neighborhoods for Halloween. Josh could remember walking this same street as a child and the memory made him feel happy and sad at the same time. It was a strange sensation.

Abby's house was a quaint bungalow, with one side completely covered in Boston Ivy. The house was flanked with a selection of shrubs representing every shade of green known in the shrub world. The heights varied, giving a layered appearance, and although tidy, there was a natural, free-growing quality. One lone rosebush bloomed by the front steps. As Josh walked up the steps he felt as if he was approaching a green oasis of calm.

But calm was not at all how Josh felt. He was so eager to see Abby again that he couldn't conceal his pleasure, and when she opened her front door, he stood awkwardly, like a teenager, with a dopey grin on his face. When he snapped out of his stupor, he stammered, "I brought you something." Then he fumbled in his pocket, removed a piece of paper and dropped it on the porch. Flustered, he scooped the paper up and began to read:

Some keep the Sabbath going to church

I keep it staying at home

With a bobolink for a chorister,

And an orchard for a dome.

Abby smiled and nodded. "Emily Dickinson. You remembered."

"Yes, I told you I would have it the next time I saw you. It was one of my grandfather's favorites."

"Mine too," Abby said.

Abby invited Josh in for a minute while she gathered her pocketbook and grabbed a light sweater. Then she moved quickly from room to room checking the lights and locking the back door. Josh stood by the door at the entrance and looked around. The living room was neat with a comfortable, eclectic mixture of furniture. One wall had built-in bookcases, and Josh surmised Abby must be a reader. Then he noticed the artwork on her walls. In particular he was drawn to two large prints in handsome, matching frames. One appeared to be a collection of butterflies and the other was beetles. He couldn't help but be drawn to the intricate design and beautiful colors of the specimens depicted. *Were they painted or photographed?* He wondered. *That explains her knowledge of beetles.*

Abby entered the living room, and followed Josh's gaze. "Oh those," she said. "My dad is a high school science teacher, and my sister and I are his favorite students. Nature rules supreme in my family."

"What about your mom?" Josh asked.

"She's an archeologist. She and my dad met at a dig in Israel. It was somewhere in the Negev desert, close to the Dead Sea. She had volunteered for a summer program. He was a tourist at the time. My father is interested in reptiles, especially snakes. Both of my parents love playing in the dirt. It was a marriage made in heaven." Abby turned off the last lamp, and headed toward Josh. "So, where shall we go for dinner?"

"You know the town better than I do. Why don't you decide? Where do you like to eat?"

"There is a nice restaurant in town overlooking the Chippewa River. It's called

The Ginkgo Tree Inn. It's a romantic bed-and-breakfast restaurant. The food is good. But it really depends on what you want to eat. If you just want a burger from the Burger Shack, that would be fine with me."

"The first restaurant sounds perfect," Josh said. "I'm a big fan for romance. Let's go there."

It was a wise choice. The Ginkgo Tree Inn was an old Victorian-style home that had been beautifully restored with careful attention to detail. As they were led to their table, Josh felt as if he had been transported back in time. The atmosphere was intimate and charming and the food smelled delicious. After they ordered their drinks, Abby said, "Josh, There's something I'm dying to ask you."

"Sure."

"The other day you said you were trying to solve a mystery, but you never said what the mystery was. I've been wondering about that ever since. If it's not too personal, could you share it with me? I absolutely love mysteries, and I'm afraid if you don't tell me, I'll go crazy thinking about it."

"Of course," Josh smiled. "In fact, that's one of the reasons why I invited you to dinner tonight, but there are actually two mysteries. The first is about an Adventure Box my brother and I received. It arrived about three months ago. Since Gumpy has been gone more than a year, I'm trying to figure out who sent it."

Abby's eyes widened with interest.

"The second mystery is about what it all means. There were only three items in the box: a watch, a feather, and what I believe is a map. The watch is an old pocket watch, and on the inside of the cover there is a picture of my grandparents when they were young. The picture must have been taken right after they were married. My grandmother was very beautiful. The second clue was a peacock feather, and the map..." Josh just shrugged as the waitress put their salads on the table. Over dinner, Josh explained to Abby about the Adventure Boxes and how long he and Erik had been receiving them. When he finished, he looked Abby directly in the eyes and asked, "You didn't send the last box to us, did you?"

"No," Abby replied, "but I wish I had. It's a great story. Actually, I already knew about the Adventure Boxes. Not the last one, of course, but the others you got through the years. Your grandfather told me about them. I think sending those boxes must have been one of his favorite things to do, after your family moved to Florida. He said it was a challenge finding enough stuff (or junk, as he put it) to keep you guys interested— things you and your brother would enjoy. I remember when your grandfather talked about those boxes, he had a gleam in his eye. Your grandparents must have been very caring people to have sent those boxes for so many years. That was an extraordinary expression of love."

"Yes," Josh answered. "I agree. We were very fortunate."

"That last box truly is a mystery. I can't imagine who would have sent it. But there were so many things about your grandfather that were not typical. I recall hearing about his memorial service. I wasn't there, but there was talk at the retirement community about playing a rock-and-roll song. That is different. You don't encounter something like that every day of the week. I think some of the residents still talk about it."

"Yes, my grandfather was a character. Apparently Gumpy planned the last box in advance and obviously had a helper. But even so, I'm left with the question: Why? Why the secrecy, and why wait a year? Do you remember any close friends he had at Rose Village who might have helped him?"

"It's been over a year Josh. Your grandparents were socially active, at least in the beginning, when they first arrived. But after your grandmother passed away, your grandfather became more reclusive. He still had friends, but he stopped participating in group events, like bingo, bridge, and line dancing. I don't know who his friends were during that period of time. After his stroke, I remember your brother Kevin visited him on several occasions. He often came with his wife and two children. I didn't realize he worked at the university. They seemed like a nice family and the children were adorable.

"In addition to your brother, there was your aunt, and also one lady who visited fairly regularly. Your grandfather was in a coma for awhile, but after he recovered this lady kept him company. Sometimes she would sit with him for hours, and other times she read to him like I occasionally did. I'm afraid I didn't talk to her much, but I was relieved to see that your grandfather had regular visitors. I just assumed she was also a relative or some close family friend. I think her name was Dickinson like the poet, or something similar."

"I don't recognize the name," Josh said. "She's definitely not a relative."

"She was a bit younger than your grandfather—maybe in her forties or fifties. She had dirty blonde hair; an attractive woman who was soft spoken. I remember thinking that there was a calmness about her, a Buddha-like quality, if that makes any sense. Your grandfather seemed to enjoy her company. I'm really sorry I don't have more to go on."

"Don't be sorry," said Josh. "You've given me a place to begin, which is more than I had before. I actually have a name now. I intend to find her."

"It shouldn't be too hard. How many Dickinsons or Dicksons can there be in the area? But I don't think the name was an exact match to the poet, so you'll have to check some variations. I am quite certain that the first part sounded like Dicks."

"I'll try them all," Josh said, "even if I have to go through all the D's in the phone book. If she's around, I'll find her."

"Josh, you said one of the items in the

Adventure Box was a map."

"Yes, I believe so. Would you like to see it? I have it in my wallet." Josh took out his wallet and removed a folded paper. He passed it to Abby. "I think it's a map. I can't imagine what else it would be."

Abby studied the paper, turning it in various directions to distinguish the top from the bottom. "What are these two black circles?"

"If I am correct, those are two enormous rocks. Each is about the size of an automobile on either side of the entrance to my grandfather's driveway. I mean the driveway of his house, before he moved to Rose Retirement Village. The line going between them would be the driveway itself."

"It looks like the driveway goes in a big circle, like at the Rose Village. What are those other lines branching out in different directions like veins?"

"Those are trails my grandfather made for riding the four-wheelers. When we were kids, he had four machines and we used to ride them on the trails. See that one there?" Josh pointed to a line that forked and went in two directions. "If I'm correct, the trail that forks right is Erik's Bumpy Road. Grandpa made a sign and nailed it to a tree. The left side he named after me, New Josh Trail. I think it was called New because he made the trail a few years later than the one he named for Erik; thus it would be the new trail."

"That makes sense," Abby said.

"It took about two days to decipher this map. At first it didn't make sense, but the more we studied it and turned the paper around, we began to put the pieces together. And it matches. It's perfectly logical. It was my brother Erik who first figured it out."

"So if X marks the spot," Abby said, pointing to a large mark between the two trails, "then something is buried in this spot?"

"That's what Erik and I believe."

"Do you have any idea what the something is?"

"I have an idea. But if I'm wrong, and I dig there I'll probably dig up a former pet; it could be a dog, a cat, or a horse. It might even be a Chupacabra. Gumpy always said they lived in his woods." Josh smiled. "I can't tell you how many times Erik and I rode through the woods with our slingshots on the hunt for Chupacabras."

"And if it's not an animal?"

"If it's not an animal, then I believe it might be swords."

"What?"

"Swords. From Africa. Old swords, more than a hundred and fifty years old."

"Please explain. This is getting more and more interesting."

"My grandparents' property has been in our family for several generations. We have one of those historic markers in front of the house from the Michigan Historical Society that shows the same family has owned the property for over a hundred years. Of course, the farm used to be much larger. Originally it was over 300 acres. By the time Gumpy came along nobody was farming. Some of the land had already been sold off, and then he sold off some more, mainly road frontage acreage where people built homes, along with some of the better farmland. The original farm was gradually whittled away to what is left of it today, a little over 30 acres with the house and a couple of barns. Most of the land our family kept is not farmable because it's filed with too many rocks, but it's very beautiful—hills, meadows, and two spring-fed ponds all hidden behind a thick wall of forest that makes it invisible from the road. You can drive right by the place and never know it's there.

"When Gumpy was a child, his parents hired a woman named Gertrude Dobbins. Her job was to help care for the kids (Gumpy and his brother and sister) and to help with housework. Gertrude was a spinster, probably in her forties, when she started working for the family. Gumpy told me she used to go into the bathroom when she was upset about something and talk to herself. Gumpy said she sometimes had long conversations. Anyway, her only family was her father who had once been a missionary in Africa. When he died, he left the swords to Gertrude. The story goes that he had brought them back from the Dark Continent—that's what they called Africa back then. I know it's politically incorrect, but doesn't it sound mysterious and exciting? Unfortunately, there wasn't much else by way of an inheritance for Gertrude. Missionaries didn't accumulate much. There was no money to speak of— just those swords."

"Wow. Are you going to look for them?"

"I don't know, Abby. The thought crossed my mind, but it seems like a lot of work. It's funny because when we were kids the idea of finding those swords was thrilling. Every time we'd go to Gumpy's place we'd ask if we could look for them. Many times we mounted expeditions and always got excited about the possibility of finding them. Gumpy was amused at our efforts. But we never found them, never got near them.

"So now, I'm all grown up, and the swords have lost their appeal. Assuming they even exist, why would I want to dig them up?"

"Well, for one thing," Abby said, "sentimental reasons. They belonged to your grandfather and his parents before him. That makes them special. And your grandfather left you a map, Josh. He must have done that for a reason. He wanted you to find something, whatever is out there. The swords are probably interesting in themselves, and they might even be worth something. If you don't want to keep them, you can donate them to a museum or give them to a university. You could even put them on eBay and sell them. But I think the most important reason to dig them up would be for the pure adventure of it. Wouldn't it be thrilling to find them? Think of the story you could tell your children and grandchildren!"

"What if I find a dead horse instead?"

"Why would your grandfather send you a map leading to a dead horse? That doesn't make sense. Whatever is there, he wanted you and Erik to find it. But on the off chance I am wrong, and it turns out to be a dead animal, then you just bury it again. I don't think the creature will mind. It's worth the risk, Josh. You are so lucky to have this opportunity to do something this exciting. I can't believe you would even pretend to be so uninterested!"

Josh smiled. "You're right, Abby. I guess it is sort of exciting, especially the way you talk about it. But, I am no Indiana Jones, and there's one more thing you should know about."

"What's that?"

"The swords are cursed."

"What?"

"Supposedly they have a curse on them, which was placed there by an African witch doctor, more than a hundred years ago. That's why my great grandparents buried them."

"You're kidding!"

"No, I'm serious. You see, Gertrude begged Gumpy's parents to bury the swords on the property. She was afraid of the swords and didn't want anything to do with them.

She said burying them would put an end to the curse. You see, the ship that brought her father home was lost at sea on its return voyage. All the people aboard presumably drowned. Gertrude's father developed a mysterious illness after arriving home and died two weeks later. He wasn't an old man, only in his sixties. According to Gertrude, he had been vigorous and healthy and then suddenly he sickened and died. The swords were sent to Gertrude by another missionary family. There was a letter informing her about her father's illness and subsequent passing. There was also a warning about the curse and a suggestion that they be buried. If the swords were buried, the letter said, the curse would be put to rest. That was the version we got from Gertrude. She believed in the curse and was terrified of the swords."

"And your grandfather? What did he believe?"

"He said the whole thing was nonsense. But he never looked for them because his mother told him not to when he was a boy. My brothers and I tried to get Gumpy to look for them with us, but he wouldn't, or he'd intentionally take us on a wild-goose chase. He said he made a promise to his mother and he wasn't about to reveal the secret. Maybe he believed in that old adage, *let sleeping dogs lie.*"

"Josh," Abby asked, "do you believe those swords are cursed?"

"No, Abby, I don't. I'm a man of science. I don't believe in curses. But I'm wondering if Gumpy didn't want the secret revealed back then, why would he want to tell us now?"

"That's a good question. And I have no idea why. But I don't believe in curses either. I mean, I really don't believe in them. So I think we should go treasure hunting."

"I don't know. Aunt Ashley is in charge of the property and I don't think she would want me poking around out there."

"Josh, my parents have a metal detector. I know they would let us use it. Can we go look? I'd love to help you. It'd be like looking for a lost treasure, with a real map and everything."

"Your parents have a metal detector?"

"Yes, Josh. Remember? My dad's a science teacher and my mom's an archeologist. Digging in the ground is what they do."

"Okay," Josh said. "But don't get too excited. I don't think we'll find anything. But at least I'll get to spend more time with you, so I'm not complaining." Josh lifted his glass for a toast. "Let's go find those swords."

Chapter 10

FINDING DORA

The following evening, Josh called Abby. "I checked the phone book. No one with the last name Dickinson knew my grandfather. I also checked all the other variations I could think of, but didn't have any luck. Then when I started looking through all the D's, I hit upon Dixon—bingo! I found her, Abby! Her name is Dora Dixon and she volunteers at Serenity Hospice Center. You were right about her name sounding a bit like the poet's. I can't thank you enough for your help. I never would have found her without you. Anyway, I'm meeting Mrs. Dixon at the hospice tomorrow at 4:00. She sounded very nice on the phone."

"That's great news. I'd really like to

know what you find out. Can you call me tomorrow after you meet with her?"

"Yeah, I promise."

"I was planning to call you later, but you beat me to it. I wanted to let you know that I picked up my dad's metal detector, and it's in the trunk of my car along with a shovel and a pickaxe. I'm ready to go hunting whenever you are."

"Great," Josh said. "We'll make plans when I talk to you tomorrow night."

After Josh hung up he called Erik to update him on his progress. He also thought of calling Jessica, which he knew was the right thing to do. But then he remembered their last conversation about the wedding and he felt that familiar queasiness in his stomach. He had a problem with her. He needed to face up to it, but he couldn't bring himself to think about it now. He was having too good a time. Besides, he needed more time, and this wasn't something to be discussed long distance over the telephone. He owed Jessica that much. Josh believed in the wisdom of the physician's motto: *Do no harm.* To him, this applied not only to medicine, but also to other aspects of life and behavior. He didn't want to harm Jessica, but he knew that he was on the verge of hurting her. Maybe he just needed a breather, or was it a total breakup that he was looking for? How would Jessica react? He had seen her on a few occasions when she didn't get her way. It wasn't pretty. Jessica didn't handle disappointment well.

Josh decided the best way to communicate with Jesssica was through email. He logged on to the computer and checked her Facebook page. Jessica had posted photos of herself and three friends at CoCo's. The pictures must have been taken with her phone camera. Josh smiled. From the photos he could tell she had definitely downed too many daiquiris. Jessica would never let her guard down enough to look so goofy if she was sober. Next Josh logged on to his email and found a message from her.

Miss you Hon. Looking forward to seeing you soon. Luv, Jess.

Josh replied: *Saw your photos. Looks like you're having fun. I'm making progress and will be back soon. Josh.*

Then he hit the send button with a sense of relief. He just bought himself another couple of days.

Serenity Hospice and Bereavement Center was located a few miles from town in a beautiful woodland setting. Josh followed a winding drive through woods and came to a building that appeared modern and fairly new. As he parked the car Josh could see that behind the building were several acres of meadows, and in the distance silhouettes of homes and trees dotted the horizon. As he walked toward the entrance of the facility, Josh thought the name Serenity was the perfect name. Inside, Josh entered an inviting area that resembled the lobby of a resort. He found himself in a spacious room with a large stone fireplace and book-filled shelves at one end. Comfortable couches and chairs formed inviting conversation areas, and each element of décor—from the wall colors to the accessories on the side tables—had obviously been chosen carefully. The overall effect was a room that evoked calm contemplation and a sense of comfort mixed with strength. Josh walked across the plank floor to the reception desk which was large and ornately carved. The wood gleamed and there was a faint smell of lemon polish. At one end of the desk stood a floral arrangement and a bell; at the other was a telephone and an open guest book for visitors to sign. The woman behind the desk had been reading, but stopped and bookmarked her page as Josh approached. She listened as Josh explained the nature of his visit, and then she picked up the phone to summon Dora Dixon.

Josh wandered the perimeter of the large room while he waited for Mrs. Dixon. He had almost reached the fireplace bookshelves when he was approached by a pleasant-looking woman with a broad, open smile. She introduced herself as Dora and offered her hand. She had deep blue eyes and shoulder-length blonde hair just beginning to turn gray around her face. Her smile was warm and genuine and Josh wondered if he was supposed to know her.

"Have we met before?" Josh asked.

"No," she replied. "Not formally." Dora continued to smile expectantly.

Suddenly Josh felt awkward at the prospect of inquiring about the Adventure Box mystery with a stranger. Perhaps he was wasting everyone's time. He heard himself say "You have a beautiful facility here. It looks new."

"It is. We opened in January. We're not even a year old."

"It's lovely," Josh said.

Even though there were no other people in the room, Dora suggested they go to one of the private meeting rooms. "That way we won't be disturbed. Would you like some coffee?"

"Yes. Thank you. I take it black," Josh said.

Dora led him to a kitchen area across from the main entrance. It appeared to be set up for families and guests because there were signs and labels to help newcomers find whatever they needed. Along one counter was a basket of fresh fruit, and a variety of cookies and muffins were arranged on platters under clear glass domes. A dining table with chairs was in the center of the room. Dora headed to the beverage section of the counter and grabbed a couple of mugs. "If you're hungry please help yourself," she said pointing to the food. "It's for everyone." Josh put a couple of cookies on a plastic plate and grabbed some napkins before following Dora to a quiet room off one of the hallways. Dora placed the mugs on the table and closed the door after Josh. Then she sat down across from him.

"So," she said, "you're Daniel's grandson."

"Yes, one of them. I have two brothers."

"I know. I saw the three of you at your grandfather's funeral."

"Oh, really? I hadn't realized that. Can I ask how you knew my grandfather?"

"I visited him at the hospital and the Rose Retirement Village when he was recovering from his stroke. We talked. Mostly I talked, and he listened, but he did get a few words in the conversation. He told me about you and your brothers. Actually, I was anticipating we would meet some day."

"But how did you know him before he got sick?"

"I didn't, not really. We met after he was ill. You might say we were fellow travelers on a journey together."

"What do you mean by journey? Did you meet on a cruise ship?"

"No. He was in no shape for a vacation when we met; nor I, for that matter."

"I don't understand."

"Josh," the woman hesitated then continued, "What I'm about to tell you will sound strange, so bizarre you might not even believe it. It's totally illogical, and doesn't make sense, but I swear it's the truth. That is all I can do. Whether you believe me or not is up to you."

Josh felt a tingling sensation throughout his body, and the hair stood up on the back of his neck. For the first time since arriving in Michigan he knew he was on the right track. He cleared his throat and leaned forward toward Dora. "Don't worry," Josh said. "These days I'm incredibly open-minded."

Dora nodded. She seemed to relax. She sipped her coffee as she gathered her thoughts, and then set the mug aside. "One day I was driving home after a morning of shopping and was hit by a car. A man had run a stop sign and plowed right into the side of my car. He hit the passenger side, and fortunately no one else was in the car with me or they likely would have been killed. I was hurt in the accident—badly, and was unconscious for several days. My husband and daughter were told I might not make it. I had a serious head injury and the doctors had to remove a portion of my skull to make room for my swollen brain. Can you see the scar?" She pulled her hair up revealing a faint mark running across the top of her forehead, just beneath the hairline. "I'm fortunate that this is all that's visible from that awful day. But there are other scars on the inside that you can't see. I have headaches, nightmares, and difficulty sleeping. And I'm afraid to drive a car." She paused and took a deep breath. "I might drive again. Who knows? My daughter drove me here today for my volunteer work. And, of course, my husband drives me around, too.

"Anyway, getting back to my story, I don't remember much about the accident itself. It seems one minute I was driving and then I was someplace else, somewhere dark. It's odd because I wasn't scared. I just felt confused and lost. I wanted to go home. Of course, I now know I was unconscious in a medically induced coma. Imagine falling into a well—a deep dark hole—but never hitting the bottom. I saw a faint glow, like a light, in the distance, and I discovered I could will my body to float toward it. It was like swimming while standing upright, very weird and very slow. I lost all track of time. I thought I was alone until I encountered," she paused and looked at Josh, "your grandfather.

"He was there, too. I don't know how he got there—I'm not altogether sure how

I got there. I remember strange noises and hallucinations. Your grandfather heard poetry. I didn't hear poetry, just the strange sounds. I had been moving towards the light you always hear about from people who have had a near-death experience. Well that's where I was heading until your grandfather stopped me. He told me not to go in that direction. He said I should go the other way, which I did with his help. Together we wandered... or floated... for... I don't know how long... hours or days. We shared stories with each other about our families and lives. He told me his name was Daniel. Actually he didn't tell me because we didn't talk in the normal way. Somehow we heard each other's thoughts—like telepathy.

"And then I woke up. I was no longer in that strange place. Instead, I was in a hospital, and alone. I asked where Daniel was and the medical personnel told me there was no such person. They said he was a dream or possibly a hallucination. Initially I accepted their explanation, but it all seemed so real— too real to be a dream. And somehow, in an unexplainable way, I could still feel his presence. I felt Daniel was somewhere nearby.

"After I regained consciousness I stayed in the hospital for a few more weeks recovering. I had to undergo some physical therapy, which mainly involved walking up and down the halls a few times a day. I was always on the lookout for Daniel, even though he wasn't supposed to be real. And one day I found him! The door to his room was open and the head of his bed was raised so his upper body was in a semi-sitting position. Although I had never really seen your grandfather in the flesh, I knew in an instant it was him. He must have sensed something because he suddenly turned to look at me, and when our eyes met he smiled in recognition. He knew who I was; I didn't have to say a word. I can't explain it, but that was a wonderful moment. It was restorative. I recovered quickly after that, and I continued to visit your grandfather, even after he returned to the Rose Village and was put in their assisted living program.

"Most of the time we just sat together and let our thoughts wander. Sometimes I read to him. He talked, but it was difficult for him. He was quite weak. Then one day I went to see him and was told he had passed away during the night."

There was another pause, longer and contemplative, and then Dora said, "I know it sounds like an incredible story, perhaps unbelievable, but I swear to you it's true."

Josh reflected on what he had just heard. Then, after a moment, he said, "I'm a medical student. I've been trained to be skeptical and rely solely on scientific data. But I've also heard stories of remarkable, miraculous things that sometimes occur. Physicians and hospitals don't like to admit it, but there's a lot that medicine can't explain. Science doesn't have all the answers, at least not yet. Some people think that being a doctor and a person of faith are not compatible, but actually I think just the opposite is true. So much happens that can't be explained or understood, that I don't know how a reasonable person could not have faith."

"Exactly!" Dora said. "The whole experience I had with Daniel changed my life and all my notions about death. That's why I decided to volunteer here. Maybe I can be of help to someone else, someone as lost as I once was. That's my hope, to do some good for somebody else."

Josh leaned back in his chair. "Now it's my turn," he said. "I really only have one question to ask of you. A few months ago, my brother and I received a box that was mailed on behalf of my grandfather. It listed the return address as Heaven. On the side of the package it said Adventure Box. Only my grandfather and my brother and I knew about the Adventure Boxes. But my grandfather was gone. He died more than a year ago. Therefore someone had to have sent the box for him. Was it you, Mrs. Dixon, who mailed that box to us?"

"Can I get you more coffee?" Dora asked.

"No thank you," Josh answered. "I'm fine." He could sense that Dora was stalling and wrestling with his question.

"What do you think, Josh? Do you think it was me?"

Josh hesitated. "I think it might have been."

Dora Dixon smiled. She waited a few moments, took a sip of coffee and then put the cup down. "Yes, Josh. It was me. I sent the box."

"Why did you wait a year after his death to send it?"

"Because, that was Daniel's request. I was following his instructions. Try to understand, Josh, I have a great affection for that grandfather of yours. He saved my life. That is what I believe. I would have waited five years if he had asked, or ten years. I would have done almost anything for that man."

"Do you know what was in the box?"

"Yes, I helped him arrange and pack it."

"Do you know why he chose those items?"

"He said he was sending you some clues, and that it would be the most important Adventure Box you and your brother would ever receive. He knew it would be a challenge, but he said the two of you were very smart and you would figure it out—eventually. He had a lot of fun making up the return address—Celestial Drive or something like that. He made me promise to wait one year after his death and then send the box. That's what I did, just as instructed. I kept my promise."

"Thank you, Dora. You're a good friend. When I go home next week I'll share your story with the rest of the family. They will all be very interested in hearing it. Whether or not they will believe, I can't say, but I think they will."

Chapter 11

SEARCHING

Josh and Abby chatted as he drove to the family home where his grandparents had lived before moving to the retirement village. He was describing his meeting with Dora the previous day. "She is a very sweet woman," Josh said. Then he told Abby the story of Dora's car accident and how she met his grandfather in a sort of nether-world.

Abby listened intently and when Josh was done she replied, "I knew they were clues! I just felt it. It's an incredible story, Josh. Do you think it's true? It seems almost too fantastic to be invented. I tend to believe her, but I don't know why; maybe because I want to believe her. Do you think she's delusional or crazy?"

"No, she seems very sane. She is quite intelligent and articulate. I can't explain why, but I believe her, too. She was very convincing, and why would she lie? Besides, *there are more things in heaven and earth, Horatio, than are dreamt of in your philosophy.*"

"Yes, Shakespeare, there are indeed."

Josh turned onto a dirt driveway and the car was engulfed in a world of dense foliage. After driving about four hundred yards, the forest opened, revealing a grassy meadow. They drove up a small hill past two enormous boulders, one on either side of the drive. Each rock was the size of an automobile.

"Those rocks are huge," Abby said. "They must be the two black circles on the map."

"That's right," Josh replied. "They've always been here; they're too big to move."

"And look at these trees!" The driveway now ran between two rows of fully mature conifers. "This place is beautiful. It's like a state park. Those are Colorado spruce and they are really big—magnificent." Abby looked all around, taking in as much as she could. "There are all kinds of trees here. This one's a beech tree. The one over there is a horse chestnut and that's a black locust."

"You certainly know your trees," Josh said. "But considering your knowledge of beetles, I shouldn't be surprised. I don't know the names of any of these trees, but they are beautiful. What kind of a tree is that?" Josh asked, pointing to his left.

"That's not a tree, silly, it's a shrub. It's a lilac, but they can get big, almost as big as a tree. They have purple flowers that smell divine in early summer. Surely you've smelled lilacs before. Are you trying to trick me?"

Josh ignored the question. "And that over there?" Josh pointed at another bush.

"Weigela."

"That one?"

"Sumac, stag-horn sumac."

"What about those, the hedge with the yellow flowers?"

"That's called...." Abby hesitated a moment searching her memory for the correct name. Then she smiled and said, "Potentilla. That plant is named potentilla. Some have yellow flowers and some have white. I prefer the yellow flowers. Potentillas bloom all summer."

"Amazing," said Josh, "I really am impressed. Did you get all this from your dad?"

"In a way, yes. He taught me to love nature. He happens to be more fascinated with the world of reptiles, while I prefer plants. My mom also likes plants. She would love this place. Thanks for bringing me here, Josh. I guess I haven't gotten out in nature enough this summer. Right now, surrounded by all these beautiful trees, I feel like I am receiving therapy for my soul."

Josh was driving slowly because the dirt drive had ruts, and also he wanted to give Abby time so see all the beauty around them. He stopped the car at the top of a grassy plateau past the boulders.

"Those trees are white pines," Abby said, pointing to the right. "Did you know the white pine is the state tree of Michigan?"

"No, I didn't know that."

"Oh my goodness! A bald cypress, and, over there is a maiden hair tree, I mean a gingko."

"Is that the one the restaurant was named after?"

"That's right. I can't believe how many specimen trees are here. That one is a tamarac—and behind it, in the distance, those are willows. Over there is a catalpa.

Your grandfather was right. This place is a cathedral, a sanctuary. No wonder he quoted that poem by Emily Dickenson."

Josh started driving again, slowly following the curved drive.

"Who lives in that white house?"

"My Aunt Ashley."

"I can't imagine living in a place like this. She must love it."

"Not really. She complains about the distance to town. She keeps threatening to sell the place."

"That would be a shame. How far from town is it? It didn't seem to take that long to get here."

"Eight miles."

"That's not far; not to come to a world like this. Does the house belong to her?"

"No. She's living there and paying the taxes. The entire place is tied up in a trust. The inheritance went both to Aunt Ashley and my mom. The two of them never could agree on anything. Ashley wants to sell the place, but my mother is reluctant. So until something is definitively decided it is everybody's to enjoy. Sometimes Kevin brings his children out here to fish. The place is pretty much the way my grandparents left it, except for a few small changes. I can understand why Aunt Ashley has misgivings. She is single and lives by herself. All she has for company is a little dog. I guess it can be scary out here alone."

"What kind of changes have there been since your grandparents were here?"

"Well, their birds are gone. Aunt Ashley wasn't as devoted to the peacocks as my grandparents were. There's only one four-wheeler now, and it's not running. The trails are almost completely overgrown. And Gumpy's head is gone; I took it with me to Florida."

"What!"

Josh burst into laughter. "Look at you! Not his real head. I took his wax head."

Abby laughed, too. "What are you talking about?"

Josh drove past the house and headed back on the circular drive toward the two large boulders. "Well, Gumpy was a bit of a cheese addict. He loved to eat cheese, even though he knew it wasn't so good for him because his cholesterol was high. He used to buy bags of these little round cheeses, called mini Babybels; each cheese was coated in red wax to keep it from spoiling. Gumpy ate two or three of these little cheeses a day. He would peel the wax off the cheese and throw the wax away. One day, who knows why, he decided to save the wax. So he started to make a wax ball. I think he was curious as to how quickly the ball would grow. I remember when I moved to Florida the wax ball was about the size of a baseball. As time passed, the ball of wax got bigger and bigger. When it was about the size of a bowling ball, he started shaping it into a head. A year later when we returned for a visit the head was almost complete. It had a neck, nose, ears and eyes. He even fashioned some of the wax into strands of hair. It was a little creepy, and Erik and I were scared of it. When we visited Gumpy, it was sitting in the guest bedroom and we asked Gumpy if he could put it somewhere else. Gumpy said we shouldn't be afraid, that the head would talk to us during the night and probably had interesting things to say. That really freaked us out. We believed him. So, of course, Gumpy moved it. Eventually he left it in the living room on his coffee table.

"After his funeral my brothers and I each picked out something of Gumpy's to remember him by. I chose the wax head."

Abby mulled over his words. "So you inherited a scary wax head."

"I did." Josh parked the car and turned off the engine. "And now it sits on my coffee table. I love that weird red head; it means the world to me. Every time I look at it, I think of my childhood and especially of my grandparents. I can see Gumpy eating his cheese and hear my grandma fussing at him for getting wax on the carpet." Josh shook his head. "They were quite a pair."

The two of them got out of the car and looked about, taking in the beauty and the sounds of the wild birds.

"Does your Aunt know we're here poking around in the woods?" Abby asked.

"She knows. I called her and asked if it would be all right to visit. She's at work, but she said it would be okay. I didn't say anything about the treasure hunting. Aunt Ashley can be a little unpredictable. It's hard to know how she will react. I don't think she would like us digging out here, and I didn't see the point in alarming her.

"Do you think it's right to keep her in the dark?"

"Maybe not, but my grandfather wanted Erik and me to find whatever's out here.

That's why he sent us a map. I'm following his wishes. Aunt Ashley might understand, but I don't want her losing sleep worrying about the curse of the swords. "

Abby nodded. "I've never seen such a variety of trees and plants in one setting, except when I visited a botanical garden in England. It must have been magical to play here as a child. Where are the trails you told me about?"

"When I was a kid they were easy to spot because my brothers and I kept them clear with four-wheelers. We rode constantly. These days, you have to know where the trails are to find them. If you look carefully, they're not too hard to spot. Come, I'll show you. Maybe you should bring the metal detector and I'll get the pickaxe and shovel."

After walking about 50 yards Josh pointed to a tree. A sign was nailed midway up the trunk. The letters on the sign were badly faded, but looking closely Abby was able to make out the words. The sign read: Erik's Bumpy Road. "It's still here," Josh said. "That sign has hung on that tree as long as I can remember. Over there," Josh pointed toward the edge of the woods, "you'll find a pair of shoes that Gumpy nailed to a tree.

I don't expect there is much left of those shoes."

"Why would he do that?"

Josh shrugged and smiled. "That's the kind of thing Gumpy did. He didn't need a reason. He probably was just feeling silly. On the other hand, maybe he was performing some mysterious ritual. Who knows? It made perfect sense to us kids. Look, Abby, here's where the trail divides. If you look carefully you can see a trail going off to the left. That is New Josh Trail. It goes to an area we named The Monkey Forest."

"There's no sign."

"No. The sign is gone, just like my grandparents. Boy... I loved this place as a child." Josh scanned the woods on all sides. He ached for all that was now beyond his grasp and longed to be transported back in time to when life was simple and his grandfather had all the answers to life's problems.

Perhaps sensing the sadness which seemed to come over Josh, Abby changed topics. "I'm going to fire up the metal detector and begin to search." She turned the machine on and began to slowly walk in circles around the area that matched the spot on Josh's map.

In just a few minutes the machine sounded the alarm. "There's something here!" she said excitedly. "Something is buried right below this spot, and it's not a dead animal."

Josh walked to where Abby was standing, and began to dig. "You know," he said, "when my mother was a child my grandparents didn't have four-wheelers. They rode horses. They also had 20 acres up north, outside of Cadillac, and they would truck those horses up there on the weekends. My mother still talks about those times. It was really remote, without electricity. They camped in tents and tied the horses to a picket line. My mother loved it, although she said the mosquitoes could be terrible. When they were up there, they worried about bears and wolves, but they never saw any. One day, when Gumpy was riding, his horse was startled and reared up. He went over backward. Gumpy tried to jump off but his jacket caught on the saddle and the horse landed on him. He was knocked unconscious. Somehow my grandma managed to drag him out of the woods and get him to a hospital. The whole time she was driving she prayed. She made a deal with God. She promised to never get on a horse again if God would please let Gumpy live.

"Well," Josh paused. "Gumpy did live, and Grandma kept her promise—she never got on a horse again. She said that was the best deal she ever made. It took my grandfather months to recover. He had a concussion, broken ribs, and a punctured lung. He spent the whole summer in a hospital bed they set up in his living room. He was in a lot of pain. It hurt to laugh. When he finally recovered he walked with a limp."

"You mean Gumpy was gimpy?"

Josh chuckled. "Yes, I guess you could say that, but it took a while to even get to that point. A couple of years after they sold the horses and Gumpy was recovered, he wanted to get back on a horse. Gumpy tried to get my grandmother to renege on her promise to God. Of course she refused. My grandmother was a stubborn woman. And she was truthful. If she made a commitment, she would honor it. So, since they couldn't ride horses again, they bought four-wheelers. By then Mom and Aunt Ashley were in college. They preferred the machines over the horses, because the machines were less work. Taking care of the horses demanded a lot of effort."

Josh paused, "I've hit something." He

continued to dig cautiously, and finally unearthed what appeared to be a rusty old wastepaper basket. It was so heavy that it took both of them to pull it out of the ground. Inside the can they found a huge jar filled with pennies.

"Cool!" Abby said. "This is big. There must be thousands of pennies."

"Gumpy always told us to save our pennies." With effort, Josh untwisted the lid and examined the coins. "These are Indian Head Pennies. These are before Gumpy's time. I'll have to check the Internet to see what they're worth."

"No swords?"

"No, just pennies."

Abby spent ten more minutes, walking the areas in circles searching for the swords or more buried coins, but nothing showed up on the detector. When she was satisfied there was nothing more to be found, they filled in the hole. Then they camouflaged the fresh dirt by spreading some dead branches and leaf litter on top.

Josh lifted the container of pennies and carried it to the car.

"Boy," he said, "that's heavy. It must weigh fifty pounds."

Abby grabbed two cold bottles of water from her backpack and handed one to Josh. Although the temperature was comfortable, the water was refreshing after their work. They both leaned against the car, enjoying their surroundings and each other's company. "Josh, do you think there really are swords buried somewhere out here?"

"Probably. I always heard there were."

"Well, as long as we're here and we have the metal detector, why don't we look for them?"

"I wouldn't know where to begin, Abby. There's more than thirty acres here. This was our best shot as to their whereabouts. It would be like looking for a needle in a haystack."

"Not necessarily, Josh. Let's use logic and think like an archaeologist. What kind of soil does this place have?"

"Rocky. The name of the town just south of here was once called Hardscrabble because of all the stones. That should tell you something."

"Is it rocky everywhere? Can you think of a spot where the ground might be different, without so many stones? For instance, if you wanted to bury something, where would you dig?"

Josh looked at Abby, and couldn't help smiling. He really didn't care about the swords, but he liked everything about this woman. He liked the way she looked, he liked the way she thought, and he liked the fact that she wasn't worried about her hair or make up. She didn't mind getting her hands dirty. Josh hadn't once seen her take an emery board to her fingernails or check her lipstick or even look in a mirror. And to top it off, he was actually having fun today, like he did when he was a child. He was having an Adventure Day! Josh thought, *wherever Gumpy is, he is smiling down on us.*

Josh rubbed his chin for a minute, still smiling. "A science teacher and an archaeologist ... that's a powerful combination. Actually, there is a spot that comes to mind. I would dig by the east pond. There's a hill on the south side that's mostly sand. Gumpy and I planted some Christmas trees there once. He chose that area because the ground was soft, and pine trees like sandy soil."

"Then I suggest we begin our treasure hunt by looking there."

"Okay, Abby, but don't be disappointed

if we don't find anything. It's still been a great day."

The pond was at the back of the property behind the house. They drove the car and parked in front of the garage. Then they unloaded their equipment and walked around the house to the south edge of the pond. Abby put on her headphones and began at the center of the hill walking in ever-widening circles. Josh sat on one of the benches at the edge of the pond. It took Abby about ten minutes before the metal detector went off.

"Over here," she yelled to Josh. "I found something."

"It's probably just trash," Josh said skeptically. "Gumpy used to have a friend with a backhoe dig pits around here so he could burn trash and dump stuff like old appliances and broken machinery."

Abby looked a little disappointed and frowned. "You never mentioned that, Josh."

"I'm sorry. I forgot until just a few minutes ago. It's funny how memories keep popping to the surface, even long forgotten stuff."

"Isn't it a violation of zoning regulations to bury trash like that?" asked Abby.

"Probably, but Gumpy never followed

rules. He didn't think rules applied to him. And he despised regulations. He said the government issued about 80,000 pages of new regulations each year. The reason, he said, was because politicians want to claim credit for doing something. They want to look like they have accomplishments. If they get a bill passed, that is proof they aren't just wasting the taxpayer's money. There are so many stupid regulations. All those rules gum things up. Nothing works the way it should. Gumpy said regulations are like suffering death by a thousand cuts."

Abby stopped. She looked at Josh. "I don't think this is an old appliance. My detector is pretty discriminating, and the pattern is smaller than a washing machine or stove."

The two began to dig. Josh had been correct about the sand, so the digging was easy. About two feet down they hit a bundle wrapped in a blanket. When they removed it, the blanket began to disintegrate, revealing plastic sheeting underneath. The plastic was brittle and stained yellow. Josh took out his pocket knife and slit the plastic. Inside he found an assortment of swords.

"I can't believe it!" Josh said. "I've heard about these things my whole life, but I never thought I'd actually see them. I wasn't even sure they existed."

There were four swords in all. The first was about three feet long and the blade had a squiggly shape to it. The metal was so tarnished it looked black. The second sword was similar but the blade was straight. The third sword was shorter, only about two feet long, and the blade was crescent shaped. All three were made from similar metal. Even the handle material was metal, but seemed to be made from metal threads. The forth sword was different. It wasn't a sword at all, but a dagger. It was only about twelve inches long with a gently curved blade. It was made from a different type of metal and the scabbard appeared inlaid with precious stones.

"Look at this, Josh," Abby said, handling the dagger. "This is something different! I think it might be gold, and these stones look like jewels. This one might really be a treasure." She pulled the dagger out of its sheathe and examined the blade. "Damascus steel," she said.

"What?" Josh asked. "What's that?"

"It's a type of steel. It refers to the process of making the blade—a very old process. It was how they made blades during the middle ages. You see how the metal is banded and mottled, like water has flowed over it." She held it out to Josh so he could examine it. "That's how you know it's Damascus steel, by the squiggly lines."

"What does it mean?"

"It means the dagger is old. It could be genuine and quite valuable."

"Really!"

"Yes, really. We've uncovered a treasure."

Josh took the dagger and examined it. "It definitely bears investigation," he said. "I have a friend back in Florida, an anthropologist, who can help me evaluate this."

"Josh, my mother's an archeologist. She would love to see the swords. Can we show them to her?"

"Of course."

They stood up and admired the three swords and the dagger lying in the sand. "Thank you for persuading me to look for these, Abby. This is truly remarkable. I can't wait to tell my brother, Erik."

They took another water break and then filled in the hole where the swords had been buried. "For now, Abby, I'd appreciate it if you didn't tell any one about our find. I want a little time to decide what needs to be done and who I need to inform."

"Sure, Josh. I won't say anything to my mom or dad until you tell me it's okay. Before we leave, can you show me around? I'd especially like to see the shoes nailed to the tree."

"All right," Josh said, turning and spreading his arms wide. "Let's begin here at the pond. This is where we used to fish. There are some enormous fish in this pond. I caught a catfish once when I was about five years old, and it was almost as big as me. Gumpy had to help me land it. The fish almost pulled me into the water."

"Is that a fish story?" Abby asked, smiling. "Are you sure it's true?"

"Yes, I swear it's true. I should have mounted that fish, but Mom fried it up for dinner. It fed a family of five. See that old stump by the side of the hill? I rolled my four-wheeler into that when I was a kid and I got tossed into the pond. The creek that runs behind the pond is Cedar Creek. It's a branch of the Pine River that runs through Alma. The creek flows north, which is unusual, and empties into the Chippewa River, about half a mile from here. The same river we saw from the restaurant."

Next, Josh led Abby to a blue barn and the former peacock house. In front of the barn he pointed to the names etched in the cement. There were the names of his grandparents, his mom and dad, Aunt Ashley, and the three brothers—Kevin, Erik, and Josh. Finally, Josh took Abby to the tree where the shoes were nailed. As Josh suspected, there wasn't much left of the shoes.

"How long have they been on this tree?" Abby asked.

"I'm not sure, but I would guess at least twenty years."

"Do you think you'll ever nail a pair of your shoes to a tree?"

"I don't know. Why would I want to do that?"

"Maybe because I asked you. I've got a silly idea," Abby said hesitantly. "Let's celebrate finding the treasure. We can have a special picnic, and for the grand finale, we can nail shoes to the tree. In remembrance of Gumpy—to carry on his tradition. What do you think? If you don't have an extra pair of shoes, we can buy a pair at a yard sale or go to a thrift shop."

"It's a good idea," Josh said. "I think

Gumpy would be happy for us to follow in his footsteps—even if they lead up a tree."

Chapter 12

A VISITOR

When Josh pulled up to Natalie's house, there was an unfamiliar car in the driveway. Assuming the family had company, he wondered if he should wait to take the treasure inside. He decided to slip in quietly, but he found the jar of pennies too heavy and awkward to hold, so he rang the doorbell. Natalie opened the door, and had a strange expression on her face. "There's someone here to see you," she said softly.

Josh was still holding the jar when he entered the living room. Immediately he was face-to-face with his fiancée.

"Jessica, what are you doing here?"

"It's a surprise, darling." Jessica said, running up to him. "I couldn't wait a week, so I decided to come and find you."

Josh placed the jar on the wooden coffee table. "I've been treasure hunting, Jess, look what I have."

"What's in the jar?" Zachary asked. "They look like pennies, but I've never seen pennies like that."

"They're called 'Indian Head Pennies,' and they're old. They haven't made them for a long time," Josh answered.

Alex tried to lift the jar, but couldn't. Then Zach had to try and he couldn't either.

"That's a lot of weight," Josh said, "I can barely lift it myself. Natalie, do you have a scale?"

"Sure," she answered, "I'll get it."

She returned with a digital scale and Josh placed the jar of pennies on it. It weighed 39.8 pounds. "No wonder it feels so heavy," Josh remarked.

"Can we have some pennies?" Alex asked.

"Boys," Natalie said, "you know better than that. The pennies belong to your uncle. He'll decide what to do with them."

"There's more," Josh said. "Wait just a minute." He turned to his fiancée, "Wait here, Jess, you won't believe what else we found. I'll be right back."

A few minutes later Josh returned carrying the swords. He laid them on the coffee table beside the jar of pennies.

"Aren't you happy to see me?" Jessica put on a playful, pouty expression. "I've gone to lot of trouble. I flew to Detroit, and changed planes to Tri-Cities. I had to fly in one of those teeny-tiny planes and it was scary. Then I rented a car and drove all the way to this place. I got a room at the *Soaring Eagle Casino*. It's beautiful, Josh, just like a Vegas hotel. I've hardly eaten all day and I'm starving. Can we go out to dinner tonight?"

"Of course, Jess, but I have to shower and change. I'm all dirty." Josh was grateful for an excuse to leave the room, but before he could take his first step, Jessica started talking again.

"I brought the wedding invitations so we can proof them. I want to get the order to the printer." Jessica paused, looking down at the swords. "What are those things?" she asked.

"Nothing," Josh said. "Just some African swords."

Alex and Zach were already checking them out. "Look, but don't touch," Josh said. "You must be very careful; they're sharp and rusty. If you cut yourself you'll have to get a tetanus vaccination and you won't like that."

"Listen to your uncle." Natalie said. "You could hurt yourselves. These are dangerous; they're not toys."

Jessica turned to Josh and asked, "Do these things have something to do with the Adventure Box?"

"Yes," Josh replied. "We were following the map—the one that was in the Adventure Box with the watch and peacock feather. It didn't lead to the swords, but it directed us to where these pennies were buried. How long are you planning to stay?"

"Not sure. I've never been to Michigan before. Is there anything worth seeing?" Jessica tossed her hair as if it were a punctuation mark, and the spectacle made Josh want to laugh.

"I'm not sure there's anything here you would like," Josh answered. He glanced at Natalie, who was watching them with curiosity. "Things are pretty low-key around here; it's a small town, you know, somewhat provincial."

"I like the casino." Then noticing the dagger she said, "Oh wait...." Her eyes widened. "What have we here? Look at this one!" She picked the dagger up from the coffee table and held it up to get a closer look.

"How come she can touch it and we can't?" Alex protested, annoyed.

"Yeah, it's not fair," Zachary whined.

"Because I'm an adult and you're a child," Jessica snapped. She turned the dagger to view it from various angles. "My... my. This is really something. And I am guessing it's valuable. Is this one for me? Joshua, please... please... Can I have it? It could be a wedding present." She pleaded to Josh with her best little-girl-pouting routine.

"Come on, Jess. You know it's not mine to give. It belongs to Erik and Kevin, as well as me."

"Okay, then just give me this half. I'll be satisfied with this part."

"The scabbard?" Josh asked.

"Yeah, whatever. I don't know what it's called—the part with the jewels."

"You mean the best part? You're joking, right?" Then, ignoring Jessica, Josh turned to Natalie and asked, "Did you see these swords? They are interesting. Take a look."

Natalie looked at the three swords on the coffee table, but Jessica refused to release the dagger.

***

It took only about thirty minutes in Jessica's company for Josh to realize that his feelings for her had changed. For months he had sensed a subtle shifting, but he had been too busy (or too lazy) to pause and take a closer look at what was happening. Since his arrival in Michigan he had barely thought of Jessica at all. Instead, he found himself preoccupied with Abby. The few times Jessica did come to mind, he literally felt ill. *A fine doctor I'll make,* he thought. *I can't even diagnose what's right in front of me until it's close enough to bite me on the nose.*

Josh could no longer ignore the signs (symptoms) that he had been avoiding for the past months. Now his problem had followed him to Michigan and was standing in front of him demanding a decision on wedding invitations. Unfortunately, all Josh could focus on was the realization that nothing about this woman appealed to him. The queasiness had returned and he felt his stomach churn. *She is literally making me sick,* he thought.

Jessica was demanding an answer to something. She stomped her feet in a dainty, playful fashion and tossed her hair to one side. Josh fought a powerful urge to laugh and tell her how ridiculous she looked. Despite his desperation Josh could appreciate the humor of the situation. Natalie had wisely whisked the boys to another part of the house. Judging from the quiet, Josh guessed they were playing video games. He wished he was playing with them.

Returning to Jessica's earlier comments about their wedding, Josh asked, "How can we print wedding invitations, Jessica? We've hardly discussed this. We haven't even set a date."

"I thought June 5th would work well. I've always wanted a June wedding."

"That's almost a year away. Do we have to decide this now? Can't we wait a little while?"

Jessica looked at Josh for a moment. "What is it, Josh? Aren't happy to see me?"

"Of course I am, Jessica, but it's a surprise and sort of a bad time. Right now the only thing I can think about is finishing school and graduation. That's my challenge."

"Meaning?"

"Meaning, I can't afford distractions now. I can concentrate only on one hurdle at a time." Josh knew he was being evasive, but he felt like Jessica had ambushed him. He wanted more time to sort through his feelings and plan what to do.

But Jessica was not ready to give up. "Is that what this is to you?" she shrieked, throwing the sample wedding invitations on the floor. "A distraction? And our wedding is an 'obstacle' to overcome, like another one of your tests?"

"Jessica, don't do this. You're twisting my words. You know I don't believe marriage is a distraction or hurdle. It's something wonderful. But it's an important step and deserves our full attention. What's the rush?"

"Josh, we're engaged. This is what people do when they're engaged. They make plans. People don't stay engaged; it's a place they visit on the way to being married."

Josh shrugged. "I think I'll visit for a while longer. I'm not ready to move on."

"Something's happened, hasn't it? You're different. What's going on?"

"Nothing, Jess, I'm the same, and so are you. Maybe we just look different to each other in Michigan."

"You're right about that," Jessica nodded. "Look at you, all covered in dirt! You're like a kid digging in a sandbox. You've even got stuff in your hair." She reached as if to flick something out of his hair, but stopped midpoint. Josh watched her features reconfigure and her eyes harden into a reptilian stare. He felt both dread and fascination. Once again he had to refrain from laughing, this time out of sheer nervousness. "Who have you been playing with, Josh?"

Josh knew he was in dangerous waters. He said nothing as he weighed his options.

"You said 'we' earlier when you talked about the swords and the pennies. You said 'we were following the map.' So who were you treasure hunting with, Josh? Who is the 'we'?"

"Abby. The nurse who cared for my grandfather. Her parents have a metal detector."

"Abby's a woman?" Jessica asked.

"Yes, but…"

"How old is Abby?"

"Jessica, this has nothing to do with Abby. It's about you and me. You're incorrect when you say I've changed. I haven't changed— I've become aware of who I really am. I think it was this trip that put things in perspective for me. You know how you say you hate nature? Well, I'm different. I love nature, and that's never going to change. I like being outside. I like digging in the ground. It's like the world is a playground. And, Jessica, I don't want to be an orthopedic surgeon. I don't need that much money. What I need is to do something I like, something that gives me fulfillment. Don't you see how different we are?"

"Does this Abby person know you're engaged?"

"What? You're not hearing me, Jess."

"Oh yes I am, Josh. I hear you loud and clear. Now it's your turn to hear me. I'm going back to my room at the Soaring Eagle, and I'm going to order something to eat from room service because I'm really hungry. Then I'm going to take a long hot bath and try to forget what just happened here. I suggest you wash up, too, and clear your head. When you come to your senses later, call me—or better yet come to see me. I'm in room 209."

Jessica stooped and picked up the scattered invitations. "I really need a decision on these," she said as she slid them into her pocketbook. Her face was flushed, but otherwise Jessica looked quite composed. She took a couple of steps toward the door, then turned and smiled at Josh. "I'll give your best to Dad when I call home. I don't see any need to worry him about all this." Then she turned and was gone.

A few minutes later, Natalie entered the room. "I couldn't help overhearing. Are you okay, Josh?"

"I'm not sure. Do I look okay?"

Natalie smiled and shook her head. "No. Not really. Are you breaking up with Jessica because of Abby?"

"Abby?"

"Yes, Josh, Abby. You know who I'm talking about."

Before Josh could answer, Zach ran into the room, chased by Alex. "Alex wiped his eye-boogers on my pants," Zach whined. "Alex is gross."

Alex looked at his Uncle Josh with total innocence. "Can you take us on an adventure, Uncle Josh?"

"Not unless you stop fighting with your brother. Otherwise I don't think either of you deserve an adventure. Besides it's getting late. It's almost time for dinner."

"Tomorrow?" Alex pleaded. "Since

Dad's away we don't have anyone to take us on adventures."

Josh looked at his two nephews. They reminded him of his brother Kevin, whom Josh hadn't seen since Gumpy's funeral. The two children were wonderful little boys, and now, at the ages of five and seven, Josh was enjoying their company more than he would have expected. He felt it was worth coming to Michigan, if for no other reason than to see his nephews again. The boys were completely different from one another, with two individual and distinct personalities. Yet, they played well together—most of the time. They were inseparable, and each other's best friend. It reminded Josh of the way things were when he and Erik were children.

"What would you rascals like to do tomorrow?"

"Can we go back to the water park?" The question came from Zach, the older brother.

"How about fishing?" Alex suggested. "Can you take us to Gumpy's pond?"

"Which would you rather do?" Josh asked.

"Fishing!" the boys answered in unison.

"Can you promise to behave and not fight with each other?"

"Yes, Uncle Josh, we promise," they both

said.

"Okay, if it's all right with your mother. And I'll need to call Aunt Ashley and get permission from her."

"Yeah… yeah…." The boys started to jump up and down. "Can we, Mom? Please… please? Is it okay? Can Uncle Josh take us fishing?"

"If Aunt Ashley says it's okay, then it's all right with me."

"Do you guys have fishing gear?" Josh asked.

"Yes, Uncle Josh. In the garage." Zach answered. "We have six rods and a fishing box. We have everything we need but bait."

"Okay, we'll stop at the market in the morning and buy some bread."

"The only thing you'll catch with bread," Alex said, "is bluegills."

"What's wrong with that?"

"Nothing," Alex continued. "There are some big bluegills in that pond. But if you want to fish for something else, something larger like catfish, you need to fish on the bottom. You don't want to use a bobber because you want the bait to just lie there. Any sort of meat will work. Worms would be all right, but I prefer sausage; kielbasa works best in my opinion."

"How do you know so much about fishing?" Josh asked. "You're only five years old."

"Dad takes us fishing," Zach answered. "Dad loves to fish Gumpy's pond."

"Okay then. First thing after breakfast, we head for the pond."

"Yeah…," the boys yelled again, and jumped up and down.

Chapter 13

FISHING

Saturday was an ideal day for fishing. It was sunny with only a slight breeze and the temperature was perfect—not too hot for a day in July. Josh stopped at the supermarket for bread and kielbasa sausage, and he also picked up some drinks and snacks for the boys. By the time they arrived at Aunt Ashley's house it was close to 10:00 a.m. Before they started to fish, they went to the house to say hello and thank her for allowing them to fish. Josh hoped she would have room in her refrigerator for their drinks and extra sausage.

As they unpacked their supplies, Josh took his nephews aside. "Don't say anything to Aunt Ashley about the swords or pennies."

Josh looked at his two nephews. "Is that okay?"

The boys nodded, and Zack asked, "Why? Don't you trust Aunt Ashley?"

"Yes, I trust Aunt Ashley, but before we do anything I want to talk with your father and Uncle Erik. They need to know first. When it's time, we'll tell everybody. Okay?"

Zack and Alex nodded affirmatively. Then in a serious voice Zack said, "That's a good plan. The treasure is top secret till we talk to Dad. He'll know what to do."

Aunt Ashley made a cup of hot chocolate for each of the boys. Then she poured coffee for herself and Josh.

"It's good to see you again, Josh. How's medical school going?"

"So far so good," he replied. "I'm getting close to graduating and plan to do my residence work in infectious disease or internal medicine."

"Well, I hope everything goes well for you. Is Kevin still in Guatemala?"

"Yes, he is." The two boys nodded in agreement.

"And what about your parents and Erik?"

"They're fine," Josh said. "Still working hard at the nursery. So far, business is good for them."

Josh glanced around the kitchen. It was much the same as when his grandparents lived here. He felt comfortable sitting at the same table where he had spent so many hours with his grandparents eating snacks and coloring pictures. Josh was surprised to see Izzy, his grandparents' dog, asleep on the floor in front of the dishwasher.

"I can't believe it," he said. "Is that really Izzy?"

Aunt Ashley smiled and nodded. At the sound of his name, Izzy raised his head slightly, looked around, and then settled back into his nap.

"He's pretty old now, the Methuselah of dogs. He doesn't do much these days except sleep and eat. He must be about nineteen or twenty years old. His eyes are pretty bad, but other than that he seems fine. Except when he's outdoors. When he's outside he keeps seeing birds that are not really there. But he thinks they're there. Then he starts barking and running in circles chasing those birds. It may be some sort of canine dementia; or, maybe it's because he's just so old."

Josh took the empty cups to the sink and rinsed them for his aunt. When he was done he knelt and patted the old dog gently on the head. Izzy's tail thumped in gratitude. Then Josh put the drinks and leftover kielbasa in the refrigerator and headed out the back door with Zach and Alex close behind.

"Good luck," Aunt Ashley called after them. "I hope you catch lots of fish."

"Mom says if we bring any fish home, she'll clean and cook them for dinner."

"That's nice," Aunt Ashley said. "She's a braver woman than me. Have fun."

Zach and Alex raced down the backyard slope toward the pond, passing their uncle on the way.

"I want to bottom-fish," Alex said.

"I'll take bread," Zach said. "I actually want to catch something."

***

It was about 2:00 p.m. when Josh and the boys returned home. Zach proudly carried a string of eight fish.

"Bluegills?" Natalie asked, as she looked in the kitchen sink to check out the fish.

"Yeah," Alex said, "and one perch. It's about a foot long. The bluegills were biting good. No luck with catfish, but we caught a koi. Uncle Josh made us throw it back. He said koi have too many bones and aren't good for eating. He said it was too pretty to let die."

"Bluegills have bones too," Natalie said, "plenty of them. I better get started." She sent the boys to take a bath, and then she asked Josh if he would stay in the kitchen because there was something she needed to tell him. Natalie filled the sink with water to rinse the fish, and then turned to Josh. "Jessica came back," she said.

"What?"

"She came right after you left. She looked pretty angry when I told her you weren't here. She said she needed to get something she forgot last night and then barged right in. She went right to your room and was only there a few seconds. At first I thought she suspected I was lying about you not being here. She caught me off guard, Josh, and before I could say anything she just stormed out of the house."

"Did she say anything?"

"Well… yes. She told me to tell you…," Natalie hesitated.

"What, Natalie? What did she say?"

"She said to tell you to go straight to hell."

"That wasn't nice!"

"No, not from your fiancée. And, she took one of the swords."

"I bet I know which one."

"Of course."

Josh took out his cell phone and called Jessica. He got her voice mail. "Jessica," he said, "please call me. You don't have to do this. Try to calm down." Then he called the Soaring Eagle Hotel and was told that Jessica had checked out.

"She left," he said to Natalie. "She actually left. And she took the dagger—our dagger. She has the only one that is probably worth something, and I think it's worth a lot."

"What are you going to do?" Natalie asked.

"I'm not sure, but I'm going to start by calling Erik. He's pretty smart. I think if anyone will know what to do, it's him."

Josh called Erik and tried to explain. "The map didn't lead to the swords. It led to a jar of Indian Head Pennies. I don't know how many, but I'm guessing thousands."

"Wow," said Erik. "I bet they're worth a lot of money."

"Yes, and that's not all."

"What do you mean?"

"I mean we found the swords."

"Who did?"

"Me and Abby. Erik, you should meet this girl. She's terrific. She was the one who took care of Gumpy after his stroke. Anyway, she has a metal detector and we went looking for the swords. I told her about the swords because we were talking about the map. The map led to the pennies. After we found the pennies she wanted to use the metal detector to look for the swords. She figured out where the swords were buried by using logic. I tell you, Erik, this is one smart girl. I never expected to actually find them, but we did, and I owe it all to Abby. I was amazed.

"One of the swords isn't a sword at all. It's a dagger. I think the handle and scabbard are made of gold and it's inlaid with stones that look like real jewels. The blade is made from Damascus steel which is an indication that the blade is old. Jessica got mad and stole it. I'm not sure what to do, Erik; that's why I'm calling you."

"Slow down, Josh. Did you say Jessica? What's Jessica doing there?"

"She paid me a surprise visit."

"And then she took the dagger?"

"Exactly."

"Why would she take it? Is she playing some kind of joke or something?"

"I wish. No, it's not a joke. She's mad and throwing one of her fits."

"What did you do to her?"

"Not much. She tried to corner me about a wedding date and to proof the invitations. She wants to have them printed. I balked and when I refused, she got mad. Then she came by this morning while I was fishing with the boys at Aunt Ashley's, and she took the dagger. I don't know where she is now, and she won't answer her phone. She might be on her way home. Should I call the police?"

"Yes, call the police," Erik said. "If you report her, they might be able to stop her at the airport, either when she leaves or when she arrives in Miami."

"Don't you think that's a little extreme? I know she's acting crazy, but I'm sure she'll settle down. Once the police are involved it's out of our hands. I'd hate to do something we'll regret."

"Josh, realistically, what do you think that dagger is worth?"

"I'm not sure, Erik. It could be fake and worth nothing. But if it's the genuine article, it's worth a lot of money. Considering the price of gold today, if it's real gold and real jewels, then we're talking about a small fortune."

Both brothers were silent for a few moments. Then Erik spoke. "In that case maybe it's not such a good idea to involve the police. They'd probably confiscate the swords, and there would be questions of ownership, not to mention taxes. I think we should try to handle this within the family. If Jessica doesn't come to her senses then we can always hire a lawyer. She's your girlfriend, Josh. Keep calling her, and for heaven's sake, try to make up. Be charming. Tell her you love her—let her pick out a wedding date. Print the damn invitations if that's what she wants. Do whatever it takes. I can't believe you're actually going to marry that fruitcake."

"I'm not. I can't go through with it."

"What do you mean?"

"We kind of broke up... I think."

"You *think* you *kind of* broke up? You don't know? What the hell is going on up there? I knew I should have come with you. Okay, Josh, what you should do now is *kind of unbreak* up. Use the telephone, email her, leave a message on Facebook—

and anything else you can think of. Tell her you're sorry. Apologize. Say it was all a big misunderstanding and you can't live without her."

"But it's not a misunderstanding, and I can live without her. There's nothing about her I like. Have you ever noticed how she flings her hair around like a lion at the zoo? I hate that."

"I know, Josh, I never could see the two of you as a couple. But your timing is really bad. You can't afford to break up now. I know how hard it is for you to lie, so why don't you regard this as giving Jessica another chance? After three years you probably owe her that much. Forgive her for this impulsive act and get the damn dagger back. Then see how you feel afterwards and decide what you need to do. For now, keep trying to make amends. If you don't reach her, I'll check her apartment. If I need to, I'll talk with her dad; maybe he can intercede. Call me later tonight and keep me posted."

"Okay. I'll do my best. I really do think Jessica will calm down after she gets the drama out of her system. My best guess is that she'll show up at Natalie's today or tomorrow, or turn up in Florida. By then she'll be cooled down, I hope. Erik, I think I'm in love."

"You just said you broke up with her."

"Not with Jessica! I'm in love with Abby."

Jim & Cheryl Pahz

Chapter 14

BAD NEWS

The following morning Josh stayed at Natalie's house expecting Jessica would show up any minute. She never did. By lunchtime Josh felt he was going crazy. The uncertainty about Jessica was nerve-wracking. Natalie and the boys had left to attend a birthday party and wouldn't be home until later in the afternoon. Josh checked his email for the third time that morning, but there was nothing new. Then he double-checked his phone to make sure it was charged and working. Once more he called Jessica and left another voice message imploring her to call him. He wished the boys were home so they would provide some distraction. Frustrated and hungry, Josh headed out to lunch and wound up at Applebee's.

The phone remained quiet during lunch, so after he finished his Fiesta Lime Chicken, Josh called Erik. Even Erik wasn't answering the phone so he left a message. He thought about calling Abby, but with everything so uncertain he wasn't sure what to say. Perhaps something like:

Hi Abby. I'm looking for my crazy fiancée who tracked me down in Michigan so we could pick out wedding invitations. She's the girl who stole my dagger. Want to help? Maybe we could use your dad's metal detector to find her. And, by the way, I think I love you.

He definitely needed to keep Abby away from this situation for now, if he had any hope of keeping her as a friend. He noticed a multi-screen movie theatre across from the restaurant, and decided that a movie would be a good way to waste time until Natalie and the boys returned. After checking the schedule, Josh bought a ticket for a movie that had just started. He turned off his cell phone, and for a while Josh lost himself in a world of vampires. Considering his current circumstances, the vampires were relaxing.

***

When Josh returned to Kevin's house, the boys greeted him at the door excitedly.

"Mom's been trying to find you," Zach said. "I better tell her you're here." The boy scampered off and quickly returned with his mother. Natalie looked ashen-faced.

"Did you hear from Jessica?" she asked.

"No."

"I kept trying to call you, but I wasn't able to reach you."

"I'm sorry," Josh said. "I was at the movies and turned the phone off. I forgot to turn it back on."

"Josh, there's been an accident—a plane crash. It was a flight from Detroit to Miami and it went down in the Everglades. There's not much information yet, but the news is reporting lots of fatalities."

Josh felt as if the air had been knocked out of him. "Are you saying Jessica was on that plane?"

"No Josh. I'm saying I don't know. That's why I asked if you had heard from her. You said she checked out of the hotel, so maybe she decided to fly home. If that's the case, she could have been on the plane that crashed. The disaster is all they are talking about on the news, but they haven't yet released any names. You might want to watch."

"I've got to call Erik," Josh said. "Maybe he knows something at his end."

***

"It's a mess, here," Erik said. "They haven't released much information, but they say names will be released in the morning. They're still bringing bodies out of the swamp. So far they haven't found many survivors, and the few who did make it are in critical condition. You can't even get near the airport now. Traffic is blocked up for miles. Josh, there's nothing we can do tonight but sit tight. I'll go to the airport first thing in the morning and as soon as I learn something, I'll call you."

"Thanks, Erik. Do what you can."

***

It was 10:00 the following morning when Josh heard from Erik.

"Josh, I'm sorry. Jessica *was* on the plane, and she didn't survive the crash. I just talked to her father."

"Oh my God! I can't believe it."

"I'm sorry, Josh; I truly am. And I'm sorry I called her a fruitcake. I was never that fond of Jessica, but she was a good person, and I am really sorry for anything negative I may have said."

"I know."

"The plane exploded upon impact and most of it was incinerated. There is debris spread over a five-mile area. At least that's what they're reporting."

"I still can't believe it. Do they know what caused the accident?"

"It's too early. There is speculation, of course. The flight was making a final approach to the airport when for some reason they aborted the landing. It lifted again to circle the airport and then something went wrong. It lost altitude and dropped right into the Everglades. There was so much destruction; it will take a while before there are answers. Jessica's parents are planning a memorial service for Thursday. You're coming, aren't you? I told them you would."

"Of course. I'll schedule a flight for the morning. Then I'll call her dad. He must be devastated. Jessica was his princess."

"He sounded terrible when I spoke to him. No parent expects to outlive a child. I feel so sorry for him and Mrs. Cabot. Call me when you have your flight information, and I'll pick you up at the airport."

***

Josh had one final task before leaving for Florida. He called Abby to let her know he would be out of town for awhile, and they would need to postpone their celebration.

"I'm sorry, Abby, but a friend of mine was on the plane that crashed yesterday in Florida. You might have seen it on the news."

"Oh my God, Josh. That was a terrible disaster."

"Yes. I need to return to Florida so I can attend a memorial service. I'll be leaving my car at Kevin's house. Abby, I don't expect to be back for a couple of weeks. Maybe we can plan our celebration after I return."

"Of course, Josh, I understand. I'm sorry for your loss. Have a safe trip. I will keep you in my prayers."

"Thank you, Abby. I'll call you as soon as I get back."

Chapter 15

CONFESSION

Two weeks later Josh returned to Michigan. It was Friday afternoon when he arrived, and the first thing he did was call Abby and make a dinner date for Saturday night. They returned to the restaurant that overlooked the Chippewa River. Josh was somber and a little nervous.

"It's good to see you again, Josh. How are you feeling? Was the memorial nice?"

"I'm all right. The service was fine, but it's not something I would like to repeat." Then, after a pause for introspection, he said, "But I'm better now that I'm back with you. It's so good to see you again. There's something I need to share with you," Josh paused and then continued, "I don't know if this is the right time, but I guess it's as good as any. It's about my friend, the one who was killed in the airplane crash."

"The one you were close to?"

"Yes," he said. "We were close. She was my girlfriend and we were engaged."

"What?" Abby was clearly surprised, and from her expression Josh could see she wasn't pleased. "You're telling me this now?"

"Please, Abby, let me explain. I wanted to tell you earlier, but it never seemed the right time. Now I want you to know the whole story." Josh paused again to reflect. "Jessica—that was her name—and I were together for three years. Her father was my mentor at medical school. He was someone I admired very much, and he was helpful to me. Looking back I can see that one of the things I liked best about my relationship with Jessica was her dad. I know it sounds odd, but he was a friend and a great teacher. He still is. He was very involved with his students and frequently had gatherings at his home. That's were I met Jessica; we were thrown together by circumstance. I was passionate about my studies and going into medicine. Dr. Cabot included me in his inner circle, so to speak. For me, it was a dream come true. Jessica, because of her dad, was a part of that dream. It took me a long time to realize that things aren't always what they seem. I've come to the conclusion that the main thing Jessica and I had in common was a shared respect and affection for her father. He was the man who brought us together. Part of her appeal was that she was his daughter; part of my appeal, I guess, was that I was one of his favorite students."

Josh paused and took a sip of his wine. Abby watched him silently. He couldn't read her expression. Josh set his glass down on the table and decided to just plow through the story. He wanted to get this unpleasant business behind him, regardless of the outcome.

"I don't mean to imply that I didn't care about Jessica. She was an attractive girl, and could be a lot of fun. Everyone said we were a cute couple, and perhaps we were. She was considered a catch, and for a while I felt really lucky; I had a scholarship for my studies and this beautiful girlfriend. I think that's why it took me so long to realize how fundamentally wrong Jessica and I were for each other. Even though we shared a common goal—for me to become a doctor—it was for different reasons. She wanted a husband to make a lot of money who could buy her a beautiful house filled with designer clothes and expensive furniture. I wanted to become a doctor so I could use my skills to help people in need. I wanted to travel abroad and do volunteer work; Jessica wanted to join the country club and throw parties. The closer I got to graduation and the time when I had to make decisions about what direction I wanted my career to go in, the more pronounced our differences became.

"I knew our relationship was in trouble. I felt it a long time ago. Nevertheless, I didn't want to face it. I didn't want a confrontation. In a way, coming to Michigan to solve the Adventure Box mystery was a welcome relief. Jessica had been pushing about a wedding date and where I should apply for a residency. The weird thing is I don't remember ever getting engaged. I mean there was nothing official—no ring or anything. She just started talking about the 'wedding' and I never refuted her or offered any resistance. I know I sound really stupid. I don't know what I was thinking."

Josh paused and sipped some more wine.

He was coming to a critical juncture in his story, and he suddenly felt hopeless. Abby sat across from him looking calm and beautiful as she listened. There was no turning back; he had to proceed.

"And then everything changed. I came to Michigan …. And I met you. All the doubts that had been simmering in the back of my mind began to coalesce. You helped me see things, Abby, and feel emotions I didn't know I had. Being with you was fun, an adventure. You are like no one I've met before. I realized I had fallen in love with you, and then Jessica showed up."

Abby looked even more shocked. "Here? She was here?"

Josh nodded. "Yes. She showed up out of the blue. She said it was a surprise. She brought sample wedding invitations. She wanted us to proof them, and choose a date for the wedding."

"Oh my God," Abby said. "Did you do that?"

"No, Abby, of course not. Everything happened so fast. It was a total disaster. I finally admitted to her my misgivings." Josh shook his head and smiled. "She didn't take it well. She got angry and stormed out of

Natalie's house. The next morning she left for home, but before she did, she took the dagger."

"You gave her the dagger?"

"No, Abby. She stole it. Jessica stopped by Natalie's house. I wasn't there because I was at Gumpy's fishing with my nephews. Natalie told her I wasn't home but Jessica barged in, apparently to see if Natalie was telling the truth. When she left she took the dagger with her. I guess it was her way of punishing me, or at least getting my attention."

"And now she's gone."

"Yes. And I'm here with you trying to explain my weak character. I'm ashamed of the way I behaved, Abby. I should have acted like a mature adult. Instead I let myself be led around like a bull with a ring through its nose. I'm not proud of what happened, and I wanted you to know the truth—thus, my confession. I need and want to be honest with you, and I hope you'll be able to forgive me."

"What happened to the dagger?"

"Who knows? I think it's a fair assumption that it's gone—probably lying somewhere in the saw grass. The debris from the crash spread over five miles."

"You said the swords had a curse on them. Do you think that's what brought the plane down?"

"That thought occurred to me; but no, I don't think the curse had anything to do with the plane crash. As a child I liked the idea of the curse because it made the swords more exciting and magical. But I never really believed in the curse, and I don't think my grandparents did either. The swords were buried as a favor to the housekeeper, Miss Dobbins, who apparently did believe in the curse. She held it responsible for the death of her father. I think my great-grandparents were simply placating her, and respecting her wishes.

"Nevertheless, curse or no curse, I've decided to put the swords back in the ground. They were never mine to dig up in the first place. They're part of the history of Gumpy's place, like the trees and the ponds. They're part of the mythology. I feel a need to return them."

"Josh, are you upset with me? Do you hold me somehow responsible because I brought the metal detector and persuaded you to look for them?"

"No, of course not. You were trying to help. And it was a real adventure. In fact, it was the best adventure I've ever had. I will never forget it. I owe the adventure to you. For that, I am grateful and I thank you."

"It was fun finding them, wasn't it? Not something that happens every day."

"Certainly not, and don't forget the pennies. I put the jar on a scale and it weighed 39.8 pounds. That's a lot of pennies—I calculated about ten thousand in all. I did a little research and figured the value of those pennies is somewhere around $194,000. That's just an estimate on my part, but it's not bad for an afternoon's adventure."

"Awesome! You're a rich man, Josh!"

"Not really. The money will need to be divided among the family members, but I should have enough to make a dent in my student loans. Medical school is expensive."

"You are a good man, Josh, but I already knew that. It was intuitive."

"Abby, do you forgive me? I know I haven't been entirely up front with you, and I am sorry."

"Yes Josh, I forgive you. But promise me from here on out, we will not keep secrets from each other. Let's always be honest. We can just start over."

"Thank you Abby. I was hoping you would say something like that. Tell me, do you have a day off this week?"

"Thursday."

"Will you go with me back to Gumpy's to bury those swords?"

"I will. Josh, I have a confession to make also. I told you I wouldn't mention the swords to anyone, but I did. I told my mom and dad because I felt they would be so interested in hearing about our adventure. Since I had borrowed the metal detector from them, I knew it was just a matter of time before they asked me about it. I broke my word to you, and so it's my turn to apologize. They will be disappointed when I tell them we returned them to the ground because that's not what archeologists do. My mother will probably go guano."

"Go what?"

"Guano. You know—bat shit."

"Oh."

Abby smiled, and then she continued, "Mom will get over it. I didn't tell them about the curse. I'm sure when I explain the swords have a curse on them, my parents will immediately see the logic of putting them back in the ground. They know all about the curse of King Tut's Tomb." Abby began to laugh and shake her head. "It doesn't matter, Josh. If you're determined to bury those things again, I want to be part of it. I want to participate. Besides, maybe we can still nail our shoes to the tree."

"Absolutely, Abby. I'm looking forward to it."

Chapter 16

CELEBRATION

Josh and Abby bought two pairs of shoes at the Salvation Army Thrift Shop. One was a pair of men's shoes—black wingtips. The other was a purple pair of women's pumps. They put their shoes in the trunk of Josh's car, beside the picnic basket that Abby had packed. It was 11:00 a.m. when they drove to Gumpy's old homestead. Their first task was to bury the swords in the same spot where they had originally found them. It took only about ten minutes, and when the swords were back in the ground, Josh offered some final words:

"Was it curse or coincidence? We will never know. Maybe with our discovery we inadvertently awakened some kind of malevolent force in the universe. If we did, we are sorry. That was never our intention. For me personally, it's beyond my comprehension why God would allow such a thing as the airplane crash to happen. So many innocent lives were lost. But I will be the first to confess that in this world, there's a lot I don't understand.

"I'm returning these swords to the one place I believe they belong. I hope that by putting them back in their hiding place, I will also put to rest any residual of whatever curse there was—if a curse ever existed at all."

Abby reached out and took Josh by the hand. She said, "Goodbye, swords. Thanks for the adventure." Then she turned to Josh, "Now for the next event—the picnic and the ceremony of the shoes."

They parked the car close to the spot where the shoes were nailed to the tree and spread a blanket. Abby opened the picnic basket, and took out a bottle of champagne.

"I think the occasion warrants something special," she said.

"Good thinking," Josh replied. He poured two glasses of the bubbly. "To Gumpy," he said, lifting his glass, "Wherever you are.

I don't know if you can see us, or for that matter, if you'll approve of what we are about to do. Some people might say we are wasting two pairs of perfectly good shoes. But I don't think you are doing that, Gumpy. You'll see right away that all we are doing is leaving a clue to show that in my heart I will always be following your footsteps. These shoes will always remind me that because of love I will never be walking alone. Thank you for bringing Abby and me together, and thank you for putting me on the path to the greatest adventure of my life."

Josh and Abby clinked their glasses together and took a sip of champagne. Then Josh picked up a hammer and a few nails. Just below the remains of his grandfather's shoes he nailed the new shoes he and Abby had just purchased.

"In your honor, Gumpy, I nail these Adventure Shoes to your tree, and I hereby nominate Abby as a fellow adventurer extraordinaire. She is worthy because of her ability to identify trees, name creepy-crawly things, and use a metal detector. She demonstrates a love of nature and true appreciation for adventure. Of course, you already knew that. You brought us together, and for that, Gumpy, I want to thank you most of all."

Josh and Abby drank their champagne and ate the food Abby had prepared—cheese and crackers, grapes, potato salad, and Abby's special chicken wings that were messy but delicious. They spent the next hour under the tree eating and sharing stories. Then after clearing off the blanket and putting away the food, they walked one of the trails through the woods and down to the pond. They talked spontaneously, jumping from topic to topic, as if trying to share as much information as they could cram into a single afternoon.

Finally it was time to pack up and go. Josh had one more place he wanted to take Abby that day. He felt a pang of sadness as he started the car and looked at the shoes on the tree. As he drove down the driveway the shoes and the tree merged with the forest and quickly disappeared. Josh wondered how many other secrets would remain forever hidden in Gumpy's forest. Then they emerged from the trees and turned on to the main road. He wanted Abby to meet Natalie and his nephews.

"If my parents were here in Michigan," Josh said, "I would want you to meet them.

But since they're in Florida, my brother Kevin's family is the next best thing."

Zach and Alex were excited when Abby and Josh walked into the house. Natalie had purchased an ice cream cake and the boys were eager to get started. Josh introduced Abby and the boys grabbed her hands and pulled her to the dining room table. Natalie scolded them, but Abby just laughed at the obvious maneuver.

"Do you feed them?" She inquired, "I mean, on a regular basis?" Everyone laughed. Once the ice cream cake was served, they settled down and the room was quiet for a few minutes while everyone ate. Then, Natalie started coffee while Josh helped clear the dishes from the table. While the coffee brewed Zach brought Vincent in and plopped him on Abby's lap.

"This is our cat, Vincent," Zach said.

"All he does is sleep all day." Alex offered. "He's older than me."

Abby gently stroked the cat as he contentedly purred and the boys tried to impress her with talk about fishing, movies they had recently seen, and a snake they had caught in the back yard.

"We wanted to put it in an aquarium,"

Alex said, "but Mom wouldn't let us."

"Imagine that," Abby offered. "I can't imagine why she wouldn't want a reptile in her living room."

As Josh watched Abby interact with Zach and Alex, he wondered: *could there really be such a thing as love at first sight?* He knew that only two months ago, he would have answered that question with an emphatic *no!* The whole concept would have seemed illogical and unscientific. *How can you love someone you don't even know?* But two months ago he hadn't met Abby, and the idea of marriage had been something he couldn't think about without feeling queasy. Now he found himself longing for a future with Abby and a family like his brothers, Erik and Kevin, had. *I can't explain it, but I belong with this woman. I know it. I love her. I loved her the moment we met.*

***

Afterward, while Josh and Abby were walking around Kevin's neighborhood, Abby said, "I've been thinking about the contents of the Adventure Box—the clues. I believe your grandfather sent you the peacock feather to remind you that God's purpose is often misunderstood—just like your grandfather's intentions were unknown to the two peacocks he tried to coax into the shed. Maybe Gumpy wanted to remind you not to distrust what you don't understand; be open to the divine."

Josh didn't reply. He kept walking as he listened to Abby. "With regard to the pocket watch, I think it's a reminder of how fast our time goes by. He was saying *carpe diem— seize the day*. You told me the picture of him and your grandmother was taken when they were young, right after they were married. But when you received the watch, your grandparents had grown old and died. That's what happens. We are casualties of time; there is no way we can stop its flow from one day to the next as it careens through our lives. But we can be mindful of each new day that carries us forward. Along with the losses and challenges there are gifts and opportunities."

"Opportunities for what?" Josh asked.

"For meaning, for a sense of satisfaction; for completion. There is the opportunity to nourish our soul, so when we look back we can say to ourselves, 'well done.'"

Josh stopped and looked at Abby. "You really have given this some thought, haven't you?"

Abby smiled, embarrassed, and started walking again. "Yes, I guess I have. Sometimes I get a bit carried away."

"No," Josh replied, catching up with her. "I like what you just said. It is something to think about. What about the paper …the map?"

"Obviously he was leading you to the pennies, so you would have a real treasure to find—one last adventure."

"Maybe Gumpy was reminding me about frugality. He saved pennies all his life. He used to say *a penny saved is a penny earned.* It may be a cliché, but it's true."

"It's possible. And the swords?" Abby asked, "How do they fit in?"

"They don't. I don't believe Gumpy wanted me to find the swords. That wasn't part of the plan. If he had wanted me to find them, he would have led me to them with his map."

"Maybe he just forgot where they were buried."

"I doubt it. I don't think he cared much about the swords; he didn't like to fight or hunt. And let's face it, practically everyone in Michigan hunts; people here are crazy about hunting. But not Gumpy, he couldn't understand the passion for killing things. He wouldn't allow others to hunt on his property. He didn't approve of killing—not for sport. He wouldn't even kill a snapping turtle or garter snake. Gumpy was about life, not death. Swords are weapons. They are about death. But I also believe that with the map, Gumpy intended to bring us together. I think that was what he planned all along."

"You're sweet, Josh, but that's a stretch of the imagination."

"Perhaps, but I don't think so. Remember the peacocks? You said not to distrust what you don't understand." They had reached an intersection, and both stopped to determine which way to go. Josh reached for Abby's hand, and they turned to face each other.

"When I came to Michigan, Abby, it was all about Gumpy and solving the mystery of his Adventure Box. But now, it is all about you—looking for ways to see you again, trying to spend as much time with you as possible. You have become my goal, because nothing seems right without you. I'm sorry I didn't tell you about Jessica earlier, when she was still alive. That was wrong of me—but I was afraid you'd think I was disingenuous. I couldn't stand the thought of not seeing you again. I hope you can forgive me."

Abby smiled. "I already have. I'm not going to hold you responsible for things that happened before we even met."

"I've fallen in love with you, Abby."

"Josh, you hardly know me."

"I know enough. I will be the first to say there are a lot of things I don't know about. I don't know about quantum mechanics or string theory. I've heard about them, but I can't explain them. I don't know how an old man can appear in another person's dream and give advice. I don't understand how a person can fall in love at first sight, even though it happened to me. Despite all the things I don't understand, there is one thing I am absolutely certain of: I love you. I know that much, and I don't need to understand it—it just is. I trust it, and I believe in you." Josh leaned forward to kiss Abby, and she leaned forward, too, meeting him halfway. Then they stood at the intersection and embraced.

Abby whispered in his ear, "I love you too, Josh."

Chapter 17

AFTERMATH

Fast forward to Josh and Abby's fifth wedding anniversary.

As usual, Josh was running a little late because the clinic was crowded. He was harried, but there was no time to waste. He managed to make it to the florist just in time to buy a beautiful bouquet. He hoped the flowers would express to Abby how much he adored her. He couldn't imagine life without her and their precious daughter. His girls, as he called them, were everything to him.

It was a hot day in south Florida, warmer than most days. The temperature hovered around 100 degrees Fahrenheit and the humidity was high. By the time he reached his front door, beads of sweat lined his upper lip and his shirt stuck to his back. He opened the door and quickly stepped into the cool, vanilla-scented air of home. Thank goodness the air conditioner was working. Abby was there to greet him.

"For me?" she asked, taking the bouquet. "You really didn't need to; I know how busy you've been lately. I thought you might forget."

Josh laughed. "A fat chance of that! There's no way I'd forget such an important date. Besides, you've been dropping hints all week." He leaned over and kissed her cheek. She smelled like cookie dough.

"Thank you for the beautiful flowers, Dr. Lagos-Ross. How was your day?"

"Busy. I don't know how many patients I saw. I stopped counting after lunch. It just went on and on. Fortunately, Betty reminded me when it was time to stop. She knew it was our anniversary and that I needed to get home on time. Where's Gabby?"

"She's asleep. I just put her down a short while ago." Gabby was their three-year-old daughter, whom they named by combining the names of Gumpy and Abby. They both thought Gabby would be a perfect choice. "We were busy in the kitchen this afternoon.

She wanted to help me make your anniversary cookies. She had fun, but it wore her out. I think we have at least an hour before she wakes up."

"Good. I need a shower; I'm all sticky and smelly."

Josh peeked at the cookies before heading upstairs, but Abby wouldn't let him eat any. They were neatly arranged on a plate, covered by a clear glass dome with a bow taped to the top. They were his favorite: Mexican wedding cookies.

"Gabby says I can't give them to you until she wakes up. Let's go upstairs so you can shower."

Josh nodded and followed Abby out of the kitchen. "How was your day?" he asked.

"Interesting. I had an adventure, but not one I'd care to repeat."

"What happened?" Josh began to remove his clothes.

"There was a lizard—a really big one—in the backyard. I took Gabby outside after breakfast for some sun and air, and found this ferocious thing staring us down. Thank God I saw it before Gabby started playing in the grass. But I was cool. We backed up slowly and came back into the house. Then I called animal control and they sent a man and woman to capture it. They told me it was a Giant Argentinean Tegu. They're not native to Florida. Baby lizards were brought from South America as pets. But they become less cute as they grow larger, so people release them into the wild. The woman told me the lizards have a nasty disposition when they reach maturity. They really aren't good pet material. Anyway, the Tegus started reproducing and now they have a foothold here in south Florida. The man said they caught two last week. They're pretty scary creatures, and I certainly don't want one living in our back yard, although a lizard might be better than an alligator or python."

"I suppose so," Josh said. "Of course, Florida has those too."

"I know."

"It sounds like you did have an interesting day."

"Yes, but that's not the half of it. The really interesting part is yet to come."

Josh looked expectantly, "What is it?"

"Well, I got a call from Erik. He told me about a story in today's paper that I needed to check out. The story's on page three about a lawsuit."

"Between whom?"

"Some guy who operates one of those flat-bottom airboats, the kind with the big propeller in the rear. He takes tourists into the Everglades to observe nature—to look for gators and snakes, and that kind of thing.

"Well one of the tourists saw something unusual lying in the saw grass and was able to fish it out. The lawsuit concerns a dispute over ownership. The tourist says the item is his because he saw it first and retrieved it. The boat owner claims it belongs to him because he owned and operated the boat, and, if it wasn't for him, the tourist never would have found the thing. Now, the State of Florida has filed an Amicus Brief claiming the item really belongs to Florida because it was found on state land. So who's right? The article ends by asking the question, 'who will be the lucky owner?'"

"What did they find?" Josh asked.

"Let me show you. You know what they say, 'A picture is worth a thousand words.'" Abby went into the kitchen and returned with the newspaper. She opened it to page three and there was the story about the lawsuit and a picture of a person holding a dagger. Josh recognized it immediately.

"Are you telling me that…?"

"I'm sure it is," Abby replied, before Josh could finish his sentence. "How many of these could be lying in the Everglades? It makes perfect sense."

"And this is the reason that Erik called?"

"Yep."

"Unbelievable! Do you think we should make a claim? Should we join this lawsuit?"

"No, of course not! Would you really want to get involved in this mess? And, do you think the winner, whoever it will be, is really lucky? Is *lucky* the operative word?"

"No," Josh said thoughtfully, "of course not. Lucky is not the word I would use. I've got to call Erik. This is incredibly interesting."

"All right, but since you've already taken your clothes off, can you shower first? And Josh, please think before you get involved with this. It's bad business. We don't need to be cursed—not again."

"I thought you didn't believe in curses?"

"I don't, but do you really want to find out if I'm right or not? Remember the shoes, the ones we nailed to the tree? And, remember the toast we made to your grandparents? You have so many blessings—a beautiful

daughter, a great career, and a loving wife—
not to mention your wax head. Do you really
need more to be happy? Think of Gumpy.
What would he advise you to do?"

"You're right." Josh said. He headed for
the bathroom, but stopped before the door
and turned back. "Oh, there is something I
forgot to mention. I've been meaning to tell
you but I've been so busy, I keep putting
it off. A few months ago I saw a position
announcement for an opening at McClaren
Central Michigan Hospital in Mount
Pleasant. I went ahead and applied for the
job, just to see what would happen."

"And?"

"Abby, I think they're going to offer me
the position."

Abby's eyes lit up, "You're kidding.
Does this mean we'll be moving back to
Michigan?"

Josh shrugged. "I guess. It's a little far to
commute."

"Go back to snowy winters, and a place
that actually has four seasons? I don't know.
That's a tough decision."

"Really?"

"No, Josh. It's not tough at all—it's
easy. I can't stand this oppressive heat and

humidity. I hate that we can't drive anywhere without traffic congestion. And the crime rate here! Do you know it's more than twice the national average? And if we lived in Michigan, I wouldn't worry about finding a dragon in my back yard, or a python or alligator. Josh, it's a no-brainer."

"Lots of people come to Florida to retire," Josh said.

"True, but we're not retired. We have plenty of time to think about our retirement years. We can come back then—if we want to."

"I was thinking the same thing. You know, Aunt Ashley wants the trust to sell Gumpy's old homestead."

"Really?"

"Kevin told me. Mom and Dad would be thrilled for us to buy Aunt Ashley's share. Are you interested?"

"Absolutely, Josh. I love that place. If we could buy it, I'd feel like we were living in paradise. Can you call your aunt and let her know we'd like to purchase it?"

"Actually, I already did. If things work out with the hospital, she's agreed to sell to us."

Abby looked both stunned and happy.

"When did all this happen?" she asked.

"Mostly, in the last couple of days. I waited to tell you until things were more certain. I wanted this to be an anniversary you'd never forget."

"Well, mission accomplished."

Josh walked over to his desk and opened the top drawer. He withdrew an envelope, and opened it, revealing airline tickets. "In two weeks the three of us will fly to Michigan. I'll complete my negotiations with the hospital, and if things go as I expect we can close on the property at that time. That is, if it's what you really want to do."

"No Josh. It has to be what *we* want to do, both of us. Is it what you really want?"

"Yes Abby. I believe it is. Michigan has always felt like the place where I belong. I'm ready to go home."

"Me too," Abby said. "When we go to Michigan in two weeks, can we go back to the place we were married, and rededicate our love?"

"The Ginkgo Tree Inn? Of course," Josh replied. "We'll show Gabby where we were married."

"Do you think our love-lock is still attached to the wrought-iron fence?"

"I'm sure our lock will be there. Maybe we can get a baby lock for Gabby, too, and attach it to our lock."

"That's a great idea, Josh. I know some people might think that locking your love to a fence and throwing away the key is a silly tradition, but to me it's a lovely and romantic gesture. How many locks do you think are on that fence now?"

"I have no idea, but I'd guess quite a few. It's hard to believe it's been five years since our wedding."

"I remember standing in that pergola, surrounded by friends and family; there couldn't have been a more beautiful setting for our wedding. I was so happy and so scared. I just knew I was going to do something stupid or make a mistake. And then the minister got your name mixed up—remember he called you Jason instead of Joshua? I almost burst out laughing. The poor man was so embarrassed when he realized his error."

What I remember most," Josh said, "was hunting down that key after you tossed it into the bushes."

"I was trying to reach the river. I just wasn't strong enough to throw it that far."

"Right. And then you were convinced our

marriage would be doomed if I didn't find the key and get it into the river. So there I am, hunting for that key in the underbrush while wearing my tuxedo, and your dad comes over and offers to run home and get his metal detector."

"That's right!" Abby laughed. "You were both so sweet, trying to indulge me and keep me calm. I'm amazed you actually found the key as quickly as you did."

"Lucky. But it wasn't that quick. It took at least fifteen minutes. I was just about ready to take your dad up on his offer when I stumbled on the key."

"You don't think missing the river was a bad omen, do you?"

"No, Abby. The key got to where it was supposed to go. That's all that matters. Besides, I don't believe in omens—nor curses, nor goblins, or leprechauns. Our key is in the river, and our love is locked forever. But I do believe there's a pot of gold at the end of the rainbow. I believe because I found my treasure—you and Gabby. That's all the treasure I will ever need."

"Josh, once we're back at Gumpy's, you aren't planning on digging up those swords again, are you?"

"Swords, Abby? What swords?"

The End

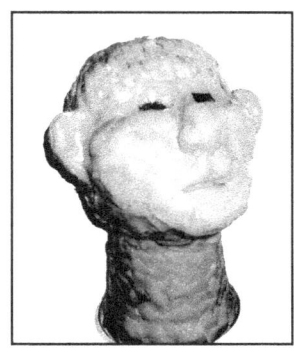

Gumpy's Wax Head is back at the
Bottle House. Though usually quiet, it
occasionally speaks—but only late at night.

GRUMPY'S POND TOUR

Now **YOU** can have the opportunity to tour Gumpy's Pond, yourself. For just $3.27 you can see all the things of interest from *The Last Adventure Box*. See:

1. The trails made for the 4-wheelers (if you can find them).

2. An interesting assortment of trees.

3. Erik's Bumpy Road. The sign is still there.

4. Josh & Abby's shoes nailed to the tree (as well as Gumpy's remaining shoe).

5. The forest home of the Chupacabras. How did they get here form Puerto Rico?

6. Gumpy's actual wax head. It is said that if you hold it up to your ear, secrets will be revealed.

7. See Josh, himself, perform an emergency appendectomy.

www.ingramcontent.com/pod-product-compliance
Lightning Source LLC
Chambersburg PA
CBHW070829120626
46556CB00002B/692